To Have
and to Hold

MYSTERY
and the
MINISTER'S
WIFE

To Have
and to Hold

SUNNI JEFFERS

GUIDEPOSTS
NEW YORK, NEW YORK

www.guideposts.com
(800) 431-2344
Guideposts Books & Inspirational Media

Cover design by Dugan Design Group
Cover illustration by Dan Brown
Interior design by Cris Kossow
Typeset by Nancy Tardi
Printed in the United States of America

To my wonderful family. You've all been so supportive over the years. It means the world to me.

Chapter One

"We put a down payment on a house today." Jessica Mackenzie wiggled in her chair in Paul Hanlon's office at Faith Briar Church, making her look younger than her twenty-three years. "It's got four bedrooms and a big yard, and it's right in town, and it's perfect."

Her fiancé, Trace Jackson, chuckled, showing his dimples. "Not quite perfect, but it has great potential."

"I would love to have you come see it, Kate," Jessica said, her honey-blonde hair swishing against her shoulders. "I love what you've done with your house, and I could use some advice."

"I'd be happy to see the house." Kate Hanlon caught a look from her husband. This wasn't the first time Jessica had turned to her for advice or confirmation since she and Paul had begun meeting with the young couple for premarital counseling. Paul had asked Kate to join the sessions to help ease the way for the couple, and Kate had immediately established a rapport with Jessica, whose mother had died long ago.

Jessica had spent her early years in Copper Mill and had recently returned to her father's estate in the hills above Copper Mill after graduating from a women's college in Virginia. Trace had moved to the area with her after getting his master's degree at a nearby university, and was renting an apartment in Pine Ridge until they married and moved into their own place.

"When do you close on the house?" Paul asked.

"In two weeks," Jessica said, reaching into her handbag and pulling out a digital camera. She pressed a few buttons and then held the camera out for Kate to see. "If all goes well."

Kate nodded. The small white house looked older but well maintained.

"Since we're paying cash, they're speeding up the process," Trace said.

Kate tried to keep the surprise from her face. Jessica had mentioned a trust fund, but she hadn't realized that it was substantial enough to pay cash for the house.

"So you'll be able to move in before the wedding?" Kate asked, trying to keep her voice even.

"We could, but we want to fix the place up a bit before we move in. After the wedding, we'll live in my apartment while we do some remodeling and painting," Trace said. "The place is small, but we'll manage."

"Dad offered to let us stay at the estate," Jessica shrugged, "but we want our own place." She looked up at Trace with puppy-dog eyes. He squeezed her hand.

"How exciting," Paul said. Kate noticed one of his eyebrows rise. "Taking on a house is a big step."

"It is, but we want to invest and begin growing equity rather than pay rent," Trace said.

"That's wise thinking," Paul said, rubbing his hand across his chin. "And a good transition to next week's session, where we'll cover finance and budgeting. Money issues are a leading cause of friction in marriages."

"I'm not worried about that." Jessica slipped the camera back into her purse. "Trace is a whiz at math and finances."

Trace nodded. "I already made a spreadsheet of our expenses, like food, utilities, insurance, taxes, that sort of thing. I think we should be able to live on my salary, at least until Jessica gets a full-time teaching position."

Trace had just started a job in Pine Ridge doing Internet security and development, and Jessica was substitute teaching in Copper Mill.

"That's a good start." Paul sat back in his chair. "The section on finances in your marriage workbook includes making a general list of all your expenditures for the past year; then it asks you to put your expenses in order of importance. Of course, your future expenses as a couple will be different from the expenses you had as single adults, so take that into account when you prioritize. Next week we'll also discuss your expectations when we cover finance and budgeting."

Jessica bit her lip and focused her eyes on the floor.

"Jessica," Paul asked, "is everything okay?"

"I don't really have records of what I spent," she said, grimacing. "I haven't really focused on it too much."

"That's no problem. Just try to recreate the expenses as best you can," Paul said.

Jessica nodded.

They spent the next half hour going through a section on godly communication in marriage from the handbook Paul had developed for premarital counseling, then they prayed together before the couple left.

Kate watched Jessica and Trace walk down the hall toward the front of the church, their arms wrapped around each other, their heads together.

"Young love," she said, shaking her head. "Do you get the impression their heads are in the clouds and they have no idea what's going on around them?"

Paul chuckled. "I suppose I'd be concerned if they weren't wildly in love, but I hope their feet will be firmly on the ground by the time we finish these sessions."

"Amen to that," Kate said. "Remember our first year? We were so excited about our new life together, but we still had to scrape to make ends meet. I think that drew us even closer together."

"You found a hundred and one ways to turn hamburger into a gourmet feast." Paul smiled. "You were a master chef even then, Katie girl. I wouldn't trade those days for any amount of money."

"Me either." Kate gazed up at her husband. He was even more handsome than the man she'd fallen in love with nearly thirty years ago.

THURSDAY MORNING, Kate stopped at the Copper Mill branch of the Mid-Cumberland Bank and Trust to deposit a check from her latest stained-glass sale. Evelyn and Georgia Cline were at their posts behind the counter, waiting on customers and cheerfully spreading the latest town gossip.

The blue-haired twins had been tellers at the bank for as long as anyone could remember.

Kate got in line and tried to ignore the chatter. While she waited, she opened an overstuffed envelope that had arrived that morning from her daughter-in-law, Rachel. As she'd suspected, it contained pieces of folded artwork from her grandchildren Ethan and Hannah.

She started to unfold one of the pictures when a noise from the manager's desk drew her attention. Melvin McKinney rose from his chair as a petite young woman across from him jumped to her feet, nearly toppling her chair, and reached for the papers he held out to her. She clutched the papers to her chest. Her honey-blonde hair whipped around as she turned to leave. It was Jessica Mackenzie, and she was clearly upset.

Seeing Jessica's distress, Kate stuffed the envelope and her bank deposit into her handbag and went after Jessica, catching up to her just as she started to leave the building. A glance at the young woman's face told Kate that something was terribly wrong. Her skin was ashen, and her eyes brimmed with unshed tears.

"Please call me back, Daddy," Jessica said into her cell phone, then snapped it shut.

Kate put her arm around Jessica's shoulders and ushered her outside, then moved away from the plate-glass door.

"Are you all right?" Kate pulled a tissue out of her handbag and held it out. Jessica took it gratefully.

"I don't know. I'm still processing."

Kate waited for the girl to go on, but she just held a tissue to her eye and sniffed.

"My car is parked right over there," Kate said, pointing to

her black Honda across the street. "Would you like me to take you somewhere?"

Jessica nodded and followed Kate to the car. Kate opened the door, and Jessica slid into the passenger seat. Kate walked around to the driver's side, got in, turned on the engine, and pulled away from the curb. "Where do you need to go?"

"I'm not sure." Jessica bit her lip. "Somewhere private, I guess." She turned her head and gazed out the window, which was starting to fog up in the cool fall air. "I can't face people right now." A tear trickled down her cheek.

"Why don't we go to my house?"

"Okay," Jessica said, her voice flat. She twisted her hands in her lap.

Kate headed east on Hamilton, then flipped on her blinker, and turned left onto Smoky Mountain Road. A few silent minutes later, Kate parked in her garage.

"Come on inside. I'll make us some tea." As much as Kate wanted to know what had happened at the bank, she knew that Jessica would open up in her own time.

Jessica nodded and followed Kate to the kitchen. "Thank you, Kate. My mother used to make tea for me whenever I was upset."

Kate smiled at Jessica. "With cream and sugar?"

"Yes, please." She was silent for a moment. She leaned her elbows on the kitchen counter. "I don't know what to do." She let out a jagged sigh.

"Come sit down." Kate poured tea and set two cups at the kitchen table.

Jessica settled into her chair, and Kate sat across from

her. Kate busied herself adding cream and sugar to her tea, then stirred it slowly, waiting.

"Today's my twenty-fourth birthday," Jessica said.

"Oh." Kate leaned forward and smiled. "Happy birthday!"

"Thanks. I'm afraid it's not very happy, though." Jessica shook her head. "Our down payment on the house bounced. I'd drawn a draft on my trust fund, and the bank manager usually authorizes my draws. I'd left a message to let him know what it was for, so I was sure it would go through."

"Oh dear." Kate blew on her tea and watched tiny wisps of steam rise off the surface. "There must be a mistake. Was there a problem with the fund?"

"There's a problem all right." Jessica looked at Kate with fresh tears welling in her eyes. "The trust fund is almost empty."

Chapter Two

Jessica pulled a pile of papers from her bag and spread them out on Kate's kitchen table.

"I thought there must be some mistake when Mr. McKinney called me and said my check bounced. I went down to the bank to get things straightened out. Mr. McKinney checked again. He even called the trustee, Henry Balderson, who is aware of my plans to buy the house." Jessica flipped through the stack. "This is the contract on the house and a printout of my account. Mr. McKinney had my trustee fax it to the bank. I talked to Henry myself and arranged to meet with him this afternoon to go over details. But here, see?" She passed a sheet of paper across the table to Kate. "My trust fund only has twenty-five hundred dollars in it. At the beginning, there was five hundred thousand dollars in it from my mother. I spent some of it, but there should still be over four hundred thousand dollars." Jessica's eyes registered shock and hurt.

Kate looked down at the paper and tried to make sense of the rows of numbers.

"Kate, someone must have stolen the money my mother left me. Who would do that?" A tear spilled down Jessica's cheek, and she dashed it away with the back of her hand.

Kate handed her another tissue. Jessica wiped her eyes, but more tears dampened her cheeks.

"I'm sorry," she said. "It's not the money, really." Her chin quivered and her hands shook. She gripped the tissue as if holding on to it would keep her from breaking into pieces. "When I was little, Mama gave me a doll that was just like a real baby." Jessica swiped the tissue under her nose. "I used to dress it up for our tea parties and pretend she was my little sister. Mama said she wished she had more little girls like me. Then she got sick."

Jessica stopped speaking. Kate waited patiently until she regained her composure. "One of the last things I told Mama was that someday I'd have a house and lots of children, and she could come sit in a rocking chair and rock my babies. She said she'd like that. This was going to be that house, even though Mama wouldn't be alive to see it."

Kate heard the despair in Jessica's voice, but she knew it had nothing to do with the money. From what she'd seen of Jessica so far, the young woman didn't seem particularly interested in riches and possessions, even though she came from a wealthy family. She'd fallen in love with a house where she could live and raise a family with the man she loved. Kate was witnessing the death of a dream, and it broke her heart to watch Jessica grieve.

"Can your father help? Isn't he a trustee?"

"He is, but he doesn't pay much attention to the fund. I'm

going to call Dad and ask him to join me at Henry's office, though. Maybe he'll be able to make sense of this."

Kate scratched her head. "That much money doesn't just disappear. It has to be somewhere," she said. "I suppose you'll find out more at your appointment this afternoon."

Jessica's shoulders slumped. "I don't understand accounting, and Trace will be at work this afternoon." She turned hopeful eyes on Kate. "I know my dad will be helpful, but I can use all the moral support I can get. Would you be willing to come with me?"

Kate wanted to help ease Jessica's distress. "Sure, if you'd like."

Jessica reached over and grasped Kate's hand. "Thank you. I know you're famous around here for solving mysteries. I'm so glad you're going to help me."

"I don't know how much I can help"—Kate patted Jessica's hand—"but I'll do my best. I'm sure we'll get this straightened out."

"LOOK AT ALL THESE DISBURSEMENTS," Gordon Mackenzie said, slapping the report with the back of his hand. They were seated in Henry Balderson's dark-paneled office in Pine Ridge. Henry leaned back in his swivel chair, his hands folded together, resting on top of his overindulged stomach. The attorney was in his late seventies, Kate guessed. What was left of his hair was white.

Jessica's father bent over a stack of documents. "The Limited. The Gap. Neiman Marcus. Macy's. Sassy Thai. How can one girl use all this stuff?"

"Those weren't all for me, Dad. I let Kristin do some

shopping, and I donated some to fund-raisers and bought some things for the women's shelter and . . ." Jessica shot Kate a panicked look. "I don't know. They were all important causes."

"I'm sure they were." Gordon cleared his throat. "And I've always encouraged you to share with your cousin, but she's an adult now. You have to be practical." He read some more, nodding as he said, "Salvation Army and World Vision. What about this one? Nine thousand dollars to the Pottery Barn. What did you buy?"

Jessica frowned. "When was that?" She shook her head.

"Sally, do you have that bill?" Henry asked his assistant, who sat quietly to one side of his desk with a fat file folder in her lap. She leafed through the papers and pulled out a document.

"Here it is." She pushed her glasses up on her nose and leaned forward, handing the paper to Jessica's father.

He frowned at it, then looked up at Jessica. "Looks like a houseful of furniture and decorating items from a year ago in March."

"Let me see." Jessica reached for the paper. She read through the bill. "Oh, this is from when we helped build a crisis pregnancy residence. I donated some of the furniture."

"I'm sure you could have shopped at a local discount store and gotten a better deal," Gordon said, pressing his lips together. "You need to keep better track of what you spend."

Jessica nodded sheepishly. "I'm not always good at the details. But Daddy, I didn't spend all that money. There's no way."

"What are these companies?" Gordon asked, looking

through the papers again. "Goldmark Environmental Enterprises? Fifty thousand dollars in the past six months. ProGreen Investment Fund? Seventy-five thousand in the past year."

"What? I didn't . . . I've never heard of those companies. I don't know what those are." Jessica wrung her hands together and looked over at Henry Balderson, her eyes welling up with tears. "Were those investments made for the trust?" she asked.

"I thought the trust stuck to blue-chip stocks," Gordon said.

"Our firm didn't initiate those investments. I told you about the requests, Gordon. You told me that you encouraged Jessica to make a few investments and that I should approve them."

"I had no idea you were talking about anything this large." Gordon shook his head. "I thought Jessica wanted to support some environmental companies. I had no idea she was giving away the farm." He shuffled papers. "I've been so busy running the resorts, you know I haven't had time to keep track of these things. That's why we pay you."

Henry's lips tightened to a thin line. "I sent you monthly reports. I called you in person, Gordon."

"Yes, and I told Jessica to watch her spending. Apparently that wasn't enough." Gordon leafed through page after page of monetary transfers. "Here's more. Fair Labor Fashion House? Global Women's Charities? This totals hundreds of thousands of dollars, Jessica." He stood and shoved the papers at his daughter. "What were you thinking? No wonder your account's busted."

Jessica shook her head and squinted at the papers. "I don't know these companies."

Gordon pushed his chair back and stood up. "Your mother . . . your grandfather would be very disappointed that I let this happen." He let out a long breath. "Jessica, I hate to say it, but this makes me wonder about your maturity." He pushed the paper toward her. "Are you sure you're ready to get married, honey? You haven't learned to live on your own yet."

"Daddy, I—"

"You have a little seed money here. Maybe you should wait a year and get a job. You can live at home until you get on your feet."

Jessica stared at her father, her eyes wide and red and her face pale.

"I'm not going to put off my wedding, Daddy. I know you think I'm being hasty, but I've known Trace for three years. We love each other, and we've prayed about it. Besides, the invitations have already been sent out."

Gordon ran a hand through his thick salt-and-pepper hair. "Look, honey, that doesn't matter. Plans can be canceled. I'd rather lose some money calling off the wedding than have you go through with it and make a mistake you'll regret for the rest of your life."

Jessica's mouth opened wide as if she was about to speak, but Gordon turned his attention to Kate.

"I'm sorry you had to witness this." He shook his head. "I blame myself. I should have paid more attention."

For a moment, he looked lost, then he took a deep breath. "All right, then. I guess there's nothing left to say." Gordon kissed his daughter's cheek. "Some lessons are hard, baby." He looked at Henry. "Let's open a checking account with some of what's left here. Put the rest in savings." He wrapped his arms around Jessica and looked down at her tear-streaked face. "You'll be fine sweetie. I suspect this will be a valuable lesson for you." With that, Gordon left.

"I didn't spend all that money," Jessica said after the door shut. "I know it looks like I did, but I don't know where it went. Honest. Someone drained my trust fund."

Kate tried to assimilate all she'd heard. The evidence looked clear. Jessica didn't keep records of her withdrawals. She couldn't say no to anyone who wanted help, and she gave away so much that she couldn't remember who she'd helped a year ago. Was Gordon right? Had she drained her trust fund?

"Have you tried to track these disbursements?" Kate asked Henry.

Henry looked to Sally, who put her hand on her hip. "If the trustee approves the disbursements—in this case, Jessica's father and Mr. Balderson—then we authorize the withdrawal. All transactions are transferred electronically."

Jessica squinted at the papers in front of her. Kate jotted down the names of the organizations on a notepad she pulled from her purse.

"Maybe we could review the withdrawals and look for a pattern."

"Are you advising Jessica?" Henry asked Kate.

"Oh no. I'm just a friend," Kate replied, smiling politely.

"Kate is the wife of my pastor," Jessica explained. "She's been kind enough to offer her help."

Henry looked at Kate and offered an ambivalent smile.

"There's still twenty-five hundred in the account," Jessica said, a new look of resolve on her face. "If you would sign off on it, Henry, I'll do as Daddy recommended and go open a personal account at the bank. Then we'll let you get back to business." Jessica gave Henry a sweet smile and sat back to wait.

Kate couldn't help admiring Jessica's soft-spoken Southern demeanor. She didn't doubt that the young woman's consternation and claims of innocence were genuine. Still, as Kate's Texan grandfather used to say, the young woman could charm a rattlesnake out of its den.

"I'M SO CONFUSED, I can't think straight," Jessica said as she drove back to Copper Mill in her BMW convertible. "There's something terribly wrong here. I just can't believe someone would steal my inheritance. Who would be so mean?"

"I doubt anyone tried to hurt you intentionally. Money is a great temptation, I'm afraid." Kate shook her head. "You're sure it's not possible you just forgot about those other transactions?"

"I'm positive I've never heard of those other organizations. I did give some of the money away, but I didn't do anything my father wouldn't have done himself. He's always been generous. I remember him telling the mayor once, 'If you're going to give something away, be sure it's something as good as what you'd buy for yourself,'" she said, lowering the pitch of her voice dramatically to imitate her father.

"Your father is a generous man," Kate said. She knew

Gordon Mackenzie had given a lot to the town. She'd also seen several plaques in memory of Jessica's mother, Amelia Mackenzie. At the high-school graduation, one of Faith Briar's teens had been awarded the Amelia Mackenzie scholarship.

"I might forget giving something away, but I never forget a name," Jessica said. "But because I don't know much about money, no one believes me."

"I wouldn't say no one believes you," Kate said, even though it seemed clear that Jessica's father didn't.

Jessica was silent for a moment, concentrating on the winding road in front of her. She was nibbling on her lower lip. On a straightaway, she looked over at Kate.

"My daddy and I have always been close, but I feel like a stranger in his house right now."

Kate felt the tension in the car shift to sadness with the change of topic.

"I keep hoping things will change between me and Daddy's wife, Monica. I can't think of her as my mother, but she could be like my big sister. It just feels as though we're on different planets." Jessica tapped her fingers on the steering wheel.

"I'm sorry, Jessica." Kate's heart went out to the young woman, who seemed overwhelmed by her recent plight. "How long has she been married to your father?" she asked.

"A little over ten years. It was the spring before my fourteenth birthday."

"Did you attend the wedding?"

"No. I was away at school." She shook her head. "Maybe it's me. She's nice to me and all, but I don't think she really approves of me."

"You've been away a lot. Relationships take time and effort. Don't give up," Kate said.

"I won't. *Rosam quae meruit ferat*," she said. At Kate's quizzical look, she added, "That's our college motto. 'She who earns the rose may bear it.' I'm not sure what it will take, and I know it'll never be the same, but I want a place in my family like I had before Mama died."

Kate had occasionally seen Monica around town. She didn't look a lot older than Jessica, although she had a sophisticated, worldly air, whereas Jessica dressed and acted like a college girl. Kate supposed Monica's position as stepmother would make her a bit intimidating.

"Keep reaching out to her. Eventually she'll come around."

Jessica kept her eyes on the road, but she smiled a little. "Thanks. You and Paul have been so kind to Trace and me ever since we first started coming to the church. I feel like God brought you into my life for a purpose, especially now that everything is such a mess."

Kate laughed. She had no doubt that God brought them together for a reason.

"Kate?"

Kate turned toward Jessica, whose profile was set against the warm-hued fall leaves outside the car window.

"Can I ask you one more thing?" Jessica began.

"Of course."

"Would you have time to come to the house Monday afternoon at about three o'clock? Monica is bringing a designer from New York with wedding dresses for me to try on. She insisted Yvette is the hottest designer this year, and

it's a real coup getting her to come here instead of us going to
New York. I'd really like your help picking one out. Monica's
tastes and mine don't always agree. My cousin Kristin will be
there too, but she's likely to side with Monica, and I would
love to have another opinion."

Kate mentally checked her schedule. "I think I should be
able to come."

Jessica sighed with relief. "Thank you! I'll make this up to
you somehow. Maybe I can help in Sunday school or the
nursery at church. Anything."

"It'd be nice for you and Trace to get involved at the
church after you're settled, but there's time for that later."

Kate feared this wedding was more likely to widen the
distance between Jessica and Monica than to bring them
together, but Jessica had spirit and determination. With those
attributes, plus a lot of prayer, perhaps there was a chance for
the two women to become friends. Kate would do whatever
she could to help.

Kate ran errands on Friday morning, making the library her
first stop. She chatted briefly with Livvy Jenner—head librar-
ian and Kate's best friend in town—then headed upstairs to
the computers.

Settling at a terminal, Kate opened the Internet browser.
She pulled out the notepad containing the names of the suspicious organizations that had received money from Jessica's
trust fund. She tried an Internet search for Goldmark
Environmental Enterprises first. A link came up. She clicked
on it.

"This page has expired" appeared on the screen.

So there had been such a company at one time, or at least a Web site. She tried Goldmark alone and found lots of links, but none to the company in question or to any environmental enterprise. According to Jessica's financial report, the last financial transaction had taken place three months ago.

ProGreen Investment Fund came up with references to pro-green, environmentally responsible companies, but no investment fund. Not even a closed Web site. Fair Labor Fashion House came up with an extensive Web listing of links to manufacturing companies that followed fair labor practices and another list of companies that didn't. The addresses for funds led to commercial mailboxes and warehouses. No owners were listed, which seemed strange to Kate.

A search for Global Women's Charities netted over seventeen million links to women's charities, but nothing connected to the name. Not even a clearinghouse.

Kate tried to track all the addresses and information Jessica had gotten from the trustee, but within the hour, she had concluded that the addresses led nowhere. As far as she could tell, none of the organizations were legitimate. The money, it appeared, had been stolen, and she had reached a dead end.

Kate sat back in her chair.

She tapped her fingers on the keyboard and thought about what to do, then she leaned forward and ran a search on identity theft. The first Web site that popped up defined identity theft as fraud that involved someone pretending to be someone else in order to steal money or gain other benefits. In this case, the thief would have posed online as Jessica, using her identifying information to steal the money from her trust fund. So whoever it was must have somehow gotten access to Jessica's computer or the information she used to access her account.

But who could have taken Jessica's money? It could have been a computer hacker, but Kate doubted it. According to what she'd read, this kind of theft often involved someone close to the victim. Stealing from a trust fund took more sophistication than using someone's credit card.

One thing was certain. The money had been stolen. Kate made a mental note to talk to Jessica about calling the police.

LIVVY FLAGGED DOWN KATE before she left the library.

"Got time for lunch?" Livvy asked.

"Is it that time already?" Kate glanced at the library clock. Eleven thirty. "I am hungry . . ."

"Good. Me too. Shall we walk?" Livvy got her purse out of her office, and then the two headed down the front steps toward the street.

"Sounds like Jessica is keeping you busy," Livvy said as they reached the sidewalk. "I heard there was an incident at the bank yesterday." Kate nodded. "The Cline sisters have been telling everyone that Jessica bounced a big check, and you rushed her out of there."

"They're telling people that?" Kate gasped.

Livvy grimaced. "They stood right at the library counter and gave me a blow-by-blow account in front of several people. When I suggested they shouldn't discuss bank clients, Georgia came right back and said that there were lots of witnesses, so it's common knowledge." She shook her head. "Anyway . . . so what really happened?"

"I don't suppose it's a secret, but I'm sure Jessica would be embarrassed to know they were spreading it around." Kate sighed. "Liv, someone drained Jessica's trust fund."

"Someone. Not her?"

"She spent some of the money, but it appears that someone else embezzled most of it." Kate shook her head as they turned the corner and made their way up Smith Street toward the diner. "I was looking into some clues just now, and I'm confident Jessica didn't make those larger transfers."

"Poor girl. That must have been a shock."

"She's bewildered, to say the least. That on top of trying to deal with wedding plans is enough to make anyone upset." Kate waved at Eli Weston through the front window of Weston's Antiques. Eli waved, then turned back to a customer. "Livvy, you know the Mackenzies pretty well, don't you? Jessica said the trust fund came from her mother."

"I'd bet that it came from her grandmother through her mother. Amelia grew up at Gentian Hill Manor." Livvy paused. "I always loved that name. It reminds me of an English country estate."

Livvy pushed open the door of the Country Diner, and they found a booth near the wall. LuAnne Matthews, the head waitress at the diner, wasted no time sliding into the booth next to Kate and turning to face them. Her green eyes looked larger than life through her horn-rimmed reading glasses.

"Hi, ladies. How are y'all doin' today? Oh, and are y'all going to the wedding shower at the Mackenzies' on Saturday?"

"I wouldn't miss it," Livvy said. "Danny's not too sure, but I told him Paul is going. You two will be there, right?" she asked Kate.

"Yes, we're both going. I think having a coed shower is a brilliant idea. It will give people a chance to get to know Trace and get reacquainted with Jessica and her family."

"Jessica's father comes in here whenever he's in town," LuAnne said. "Leaves good tips too. That wife of his is a little too uppity to eat at a diner, though. There's something strange about that one."

Kate leaned forward. "What do you mean?"

"Let's just say there were some raised eyebrows when Gordon Mackenzie went off and married a girl half his age. Let's just leave it at that."

A bell dinged in the service window, and LuAnne stood and straightened her white apron. "Gotta get back to work, I guess." She pulled out a pad and a pen.

"What'll you have today? Today's special is to die for. J.B. fried up some ham and fixed black-eyed peas and collard greens. Loretta made fresh rhubarb pie. It'll make your tongue stand up and sing hallelujah."

"I'll have that," Livvy said.

"Make that two."

LuAnne grinned. "You got it." She hurried off to turn in their orders.

"What's your impression of Jessica's stepmother?" Kate asked as soon as LuAnne was out of earshot.

"Monica seems nice enough." Livvy tapped her fingers on the tabletop. "As LuAnne said, there was some speculation when she first married Gordon . . ." Livvy's voice trailed off.

"Because of the age difference?" Kate prompted.

"That and the money. She came from a different world, in so many ways."

LuAnne returned a moment later and placed glasses of water on the table. Livvy waited until she walked away before she continued. "I'm sure the stories were exaggerated. You know how people talk. But it seems she spent a lot of money right at first, redecorating Gentian Hill Manor and buying fancy new cars and such, and it caught the attention of some folks in town."

"Are you saying Monica married Gordon for his money?" Kate took a sip of the icy water from the glass in front of her.

"I think it's hard to know why anyone does anything," Livvy said, her voice kind. "Often, love brings together people we would never expect." She wrapped her fingers around her glass. "But Monica grew up without a lot and does appreciate the finer things in life. There are some who suspect that money had more to do with Monica's motivations than she would ever admit."

Chapter Three

I knew this shower would be an event," Renee Lambert said as she smoothed her hot-pink blouse, then gazed lovingly at her French-manicured nails. Her dog Kisses was asleep in his carrier at her feet. "Monica's the only other woman in town besides me who knows how to throw a good party."

Renee was one of Copper Mill's most social butterflies and a member of the Faith Briar church board. The woman was meddlesome to say the least, and she always had an opinion, but over time, she had become Kate's friend.

A soft breeze ruffled the floral scarf tied around Kate's neck as she stood next to Renee and Livvy on the Mackenzies' backyard patio. The warm air carried scents of lemon thyme, basil, and rosemary mixed with the sweet florals of petunias and geraniums that spilled out of marble urns around the patio. Wisteria vines climbed the marbled columns supporting the second-story balcony off the back of the mansion.

"Monica does do a good job entertaining," Livvy added, smiling.

"Certainly. The Chattanooga and Knoxville newspapers always cover her charity events, you know." Renee took a canapé from a passing tray and bit into it. "I've been to most of them myself. Monica and I are dear friends, you know." She patted her carefully coiffed, salon-blonde hair.

Kate stifled a laugh. Monica was young enough to be Renee's daughter, but it did make sense that Renee would know the Mackenzies. Renee and Monica had common interests, and both were active in Harrington County's high-society circles.

Round tables on the patio were decked out in crisp white linens and exquisite baskets of pale green cymbidium orchids, chinaberries, and round, waxy leaves. Cloth napkins and gleaming silverware graced each place setting. Near the buffet tables, a large tub held ice and every variety of flavored waters, soft drinks, and sparkling cider.

Monica Mackenzie came out of the house. She looked stunning in a red-silk shrug over a tube top and a long, raspberry, orange, olive green, and black floral skirt. Her blonde hair was pulled back in a French twist, held in place by a large ornate gemstone clasp, showcasing her diamond-studded earrings. Tall and slender, she looked as if she'd just stepped out of the pages of *Glamour* magazine.

"Welcome, ladies," Monica said, walking toward the edge of the patio where Kate, Livvy, and Renee stood.

"What lovely decorations," Kate said to Monica, looking around at the patio adornments. She introduced herself and shook Monica's hand. "It's so nice of you to host such a beautiful shower for Jessica. I know she must be thrilled."

"It's no trouble at all. We love to entertain. That's why we have this," Monica said, waving her arm expansively.

The patio was large and beautifully furnished and had a state-of-the-art outdoor kitchen. Gordon Mackenzie owned a chain of high-end resorts, and the patio looked as if it could have been at one of his hotels.

"It's exquisite." Livvy nodded her approval. "I don't remember this patio. Is this flagstone? You must have put in a ton of work to make it look like this."

"We've totally redone the backyard in the past year," Monica said, smiling. "It was a lot of work, but it's worth it. I just love being able to have people over."

"I'm sure you throw wonderful parties." Kate searched Monica's face, looking for some hint of guilt about the trust fund, but Monica's smile remained fixed as she played the role of the perfect hostess. A moment later, Gordon called her from inside the house, and Monica hurried away.

Livvy excused herself to find Danny, and Renee wandered off to talk to Paul about getting new choir robes, so Kate wandered to the edge of the patio overlooking the valley.

Soft classical music accompanied hushed voices in the background. In the distance, a horse whinnied. Glancing around the expansive landscape of Gentian Hill Manor, Kate felt as if she'd been transported to a distant place, far from the western slope of the Tennessee Appalachian Mountains. Livvy had said it reminded her of an English country estate, but Kate thought the scene was more like a hillside in Tuscany.

Beyond the patio to the south, a carpet of manicured lawn sloped down through an apple orchard heavy with bright red fruit. Below the orchard, the land dropped away to a terrace of silvery green olive trees. Past that, curving back toward the west, a Greek-styled amphitheater was cut into the hillside. Quarried stone steps formed semicircular tiers of seats leading down to a stage. Copper Mill Creek and the town below filled in the background.

A perfect setting for a party. *An unlikely setting for a crime, though,* Kate thought as Jessica's pilfered trust fund came to mind. And yet someone within the sphere of this lovely estate could be the thief.

"What do you think?" a soft voice asked behind her.

Startled from her reverie, Kate glanced over her shoulder and saw the petite young woman who stood half a foot shorter than Kate.

"I was just thinking about you," Kate said. "It's beautiful. I can see why you want to get married here."

Wisps of Jessica Mackenzie's hair blew across her face. She tucked the strands behind her ears, and Kate noticed the hint of sadness clouding her blue eyes.

"It's changed a lot since my mother died."

Kate smiled. "How so?"

"Mama grew the most amazing roses," Jessica said, sighing. "They smelled so sweet. We had a gazebo over there." She pointed toward the north where several levels of terraced land held long arbors overgrown and shaded by intertwined grapevines.

Clusters of grapes so dark they looked black hung down through the lattice framing. Four levels down, next to the amphitheater stage with its Grecian columns, a waterfall cascaded over a jumble of marble slabs into a large rectangular marble pool. Beyond, royal blue flowers carpeted the hillside.

Kate guessed they were wild gentians, which grew in the area, although such a profusion of flowers must have been cultivated to look so perfect.

"We had a porch swing with big soft cushions in the gazebo. I used to sit there and read while Mama and Bertie, our gardener, worked on her roses. Mama had old-fashioned gardens with snapdragons and sweet peas and daisies, and a kitchen garden too." Jessica let out a deep sigh. Kate wasn't sure if it held nostalgia or sorrow, but she suspected both.

"Obviously, Monica has gardens too," Jessica said after a pause, "but they're different. Mama's flowers are all gone, except the blue gentians. I think Monica had to leave them 'cause my grandmother named the house after them. But I'm glad at least they're still here. I have a feeling Bertie insisted on it."

"Did Bertie help out with the renovations?"

"No. Even though he retired a few years back, he offered to help, but Anthony—he's the new gardener—and Monica refused." Jessica shrugged. "I felt bad for Bertie. He and his wife, Flora, retired after Monica came, and I never understood why. They're still active and sometimes seem to miss their time here." She looked around the backyard. "They're both coming today."

"I imagine it's been hard for you to see all the changes they've made," Kate said, "but I'm sure your father wanted Monica to feel like this is her home."

Jessica sighed. "I guess. I used to dream of getting married in the gazebo. But the landscaping *is* pretty. It's just . . . different."

Planning her wedding was obviously bringing bittersweet

memories of her mother to the forefront of Jessica's mind. Kate decided to change the subject.

"So the wedding will be held here on the patio?"

Jessica nodded.

"Monica is arguing for the amphitheater, but I think that's overkill. I mean, we're not trying to put on a show. We just want a simple ceremony."

"How many people will be attending?"

"Trace and I sent out a hundred and twenty invitations, but Monica sent that many more. Her parties are legendary, so I expect a crowd. She plans to put tables around the pool for a dinner reception. That'll be pretty."

"I gather Monica's helping you plan the wedding?" Kate asked.

"That's one way to put it." Jessica laughed.

Kate raised an eyebrow.

"It's fine. I didn't have time to do much planning with finals and moving home and all. She'll put together a nice party."

Kate turned her head and saw Jessica's father off to one side talking with Paul and Trace and a couple of other men. She didn't see Monica anywhere.

"I'm just thinking of Trace's family. He grew up on a farm in Kansas, and all of his relatives are coming for the wedding. I don't want them to be uncomfortable, you know?"

Trace turned toward them, and Jessica waved at him.

"Go on," Kate said. "We'll talk later."

Jessica smiled her thanks, then went to meet Trace, who was walking toward her. He put his arm around Jessica's waist, and she leaned her head against his shoulder. Kate couldn't help but smile at the happy couple.

Chapter Four

Kate piled greens onto her plate, trying to identify the dressing. She heard a screech and looked up in time to see Jessica jump up from her seat and launch herself into the arms of a tall, dark, very handsome stranger. Trace looked up at the same time and stood up. From the expression of surprise and confusion on his face, he didn't know the stranger either, but the man leaned down and kissed Jessica squarely on the cheek. Trace put down his napkin and walked toward his fiancée.

Unfazed, Jessica turned to Trace, her arm still around the newcomer. She introduced them and the men shook hands, but neither man smiled.

"Didn't know he was coming," a man's voice murmured behind her.

Kate turned to see a tall, gaunt elderly man staring at the threesome. He glanced down at Kate and Paul, who had just joined Jessica. "I'm Bertie." He held out his hand, and Paul shook it. "Handsome fella, isn't he, and he's done right well for himself. I always figured he'd be the one to marry Miss Jessica. Maybe he came to claim her."

"Really?" Kate raised an eyebrow. "They seem to be old friends."

"Yes, indeed. Brian's father was the stable master here at Gentian Hill Manor when Brian was just a boy. Miss Jessica used to follow Brian around like a little puppy dog. He was older, but he treated her like a little princess and taught her to ride. After the missus died, Brian and his father moved out west near one of Mr. Mackenzie's resorts. Now they have a fine horse ranch where they train thoroughbreds." He slowly nodded his head. "He and Miss Jessica used to spend hours with the horses."

Gordon and Monica got up to greet Brian, then escorted him to their table. They moved over, giving him a seat next to Jessica. The four of them began a lively conversation. Poor Trace seemed forgotten at his own wedding shower.

Kate and Paul went to sit next to the Jenners at a table looking out toward the valley. Large umbrellas shaded the tables from the late-afternoon sun. The band was still playing, but the music had become more subdued.

"That's Brian Levy," Livvy said, leaning in toward Kate. "I remember him when he was just a kid, maybe eleven or twelve. He came to my Sunday-school class once in a while, although most mornings he stayed home to help his father with the Mackenzies' horses. He was a quiet young man. He and his father moved soon after Amelia died."

Kate looked over at the man in time to see a tall, model-slender young woman come up behind him and wrap her arms around his neck. He looked up at her. She gave him a flirty grin, then she glanced sideways at Jessica with a look that Kate thought presented a challenge.

"Who's that?" Kate asked.

"That's Kristin Holloway, Jessica's cousin," Livvy said. "She used to spend a lot of time here."

"Ah . . ." Kate watched the cousins. Jessica was smiling at Kristin, but Kristin was practically ignoring her cousin. All of her attention was focused on Brian. It wasn't hard for Kate to deduce that Kristin had a crush on Brian. Kate wondered about the relationship between the two cousins. Could Kristin be the trust-fund thief?

Kate's thoughts were interrupted by the ringing of a bell. Kate looked up to see Renee Lambert standing by the edge of the patio, trying to get everyone's attention.

"It's time for door prizes," she said, clapping her hands.

The older woman looked poised in high heels, silky slacks, and sequined top. She was in her element, Kate decided, watching with amusement.

"And the lucky winner of a spa day is . . ." Renee drawled in her most dramatic voice, fishing for a name in a crystal bowl. She drew out a slip of paper and unfolded it.

"Kate Hanlon!" Renee announced. "You'll spend a day at the Hamilton Springs spa with the Mackenzie girls, a gift from Monica and Gordon. Congratulations," she said.

"Me?" Kate said. "I'm delighted!"

Jessica smiled at Kate from across the patio and gave her a thumbs-up. Trace sat on one side of her; Brian sat on the other side, with Kristin next to him, apparently doing her best to occupy his attention.

Renee gave away several more door prizes. The last prize went to Danny Jenner for a day of golf with Gordon and Trace.

"Looks like we got the grand prizes," he told Kate across the table.

"We certainly did," Kate said, laughing. She didn't spend much time at the spa, but she was looking forward to a nice relaxing massage.

"Time to open the gifts," Renee announced from a central spot on the patio.

As she orchestrated the proceedings, having everyone move into a circle around the couple, servers brought out a large cake decorated with pink roses. The housekeeper brought out stacks of gold-edged Wedgwood dessert plates. Monica cut neat squares of cake, and Kate and Livvy passed out the desserts while Jessica opened her presents. She ripped into a package wrapped in heavy gold paper with a large gold and white bow. She folded back the paper.

"Oh!" Jessica looked over at Monica. "Thank you!" She held up a gold-framed print of Gentian Hill Manor with two horses and riders posed in front of the house. "It's Dad and me," she said. "It's perfect!"

"Your father thought you'd like it," Monica said simply.

Jessica's smile slipped a slight notch, but she nodded. "He's right. Thank you." She passed it to Trace, who looked at it and made an appreciative noise.

Kate wondered if the stepmother realized she'd distanced herself from the gift or if she'd done it on purpose. She couldn't figure out Monica Mackenzie. She had a perfect smile as she moved among the guests. Too perfect, perhaps. Her smooth, tanned skin and composed features never creased. Kate hadn't noticed any laugh lines, or any lines at all, in the stylish woman's countenance.

Kate watched her for a moment, until Monica caught her staring and she had to look away. Jessica didn't appear to be suspicious of her stepmother, but then she seemed to trust everyone.

"Won't she make a lovely bride?" a voice close to Kate said with a clipped English accent.

Kate blinked. Turning around, she saw a sturdy older woman wearing a paisley dress and a pillbox hat with a little netting around it.

"You'd be Kate Hanlon," the woman said. "Jessica has told me all about you. I'm Flora Ripple; I'm Bertie's wife. I was also Mrs. Amelia's housekeeper," she said.

"How nice to meet you," Kate said.

"Jessica told me how you're helping her. I'm glad. She needs it," Flora said, staring at the young couple.

Kate wondered if Flora was referring to Jessica's missing trust-fund money or the wedding, but she didn't ask. Either way, she definitely wanted to talk to the retired housekeeper and discover what the woman might know.

"Have Jessica bring you to visit me soon," Flora said, casting a furtive glance around the patio. "We need to talk."

Out of the corner of her eye, Kate saw Gordon watching them from across the patio.

Chapter Five

Paul came out of the Copper Mill First Baptist Church Monday afternoon, where he'd met with Pastor Bobby Evans about a community project. The breeze had shifted, bringing a chill from the north. Paul had parked in the lot across the street. As he stepped up on the curb, Trace Jackson came out of the Cumberland Realty office and turned toward him with a stack of papers in his hands.

"Hi, Trace. How are you?" Paul glanced at his watch: 2:50. "You must have gotten off work early today."

"Hey, Pastor. I did. I had some business to conduct." He waited until he got up next to Paul to elaborate.

"Jessica was so devastated about losing the house, I decided to surprise her. Don't tell her, but I plan to give her the house as a wedding present."

Paul schooled his features to hide his shock. "Wow"—he took a deep breath—"that's quite a gift," he said slowly. "Jessica doesn't know what you're planning?"

Trace shook his head.

"If I pulled a surprise like that on Kate," Paul added, "I'd sure have some explaining to do . . ."

Trace chuckled. "I know she'll be excited. She wants that house. We both do. And the agent said I should qualify for a loan. Of course, I just started my job, but she says that shouldn't matter. I had enough of a down payment to secure the loan."

"Ah. Well, I suppose this will give us plenty to talk about tomorrow at our counseling session." Paul shook his head and bit back the urge to tell Trace he needed to talk to Jessica before finalizing the loan. "Remember, we'll be discussing spending and saving money as a couple."

"Well . . ." Trace grimaced. "The thing is, Jessica doesn't really realize how much I had saved up. It doesn't compare to what was in her trust, so I figured I'd put it away for the future, but now we need it. But I can't tell her now, or it won't be a surprise." He looked sheepish. "Is there any way you could not bring it up tomorrow?"

Paul hesitated. Should he keep silent about this? "I understand your desire to surprise Jessica with such a special gift," Paul said slowly, "but buying a house is a big decision. Are you positive you don't want to discuss it with her first?"

"I'm sure." Trace took a step back. "I know she's going to be so excited." He glanced down at his watch and started toward his car. "I'd better get going. See you tomorrow night."

Paul raised his hand. "See you," he called back, watching Trace jog toward his car.

Paul felt a twinge of concern for his young friend. The man's desire to please his fiancée was admirable, but Trace was talking about a huge debt, not a piece of jewelry. He had only just started a new job, and Jessica was substitute teaching. Would that provide enough income to cover the financial burden of home ownership?

It also seemed odd to Paul that Trace had been willing to let Jessica spend her trust fund without mentioning that he could help. Something about it didn't seem right.

He prayed for wisdom in leading and advising this young couple into truth and unity and reliance on the Lord. It was a tall order.

HELEN, THE MACKENZIES' new housekeeper, led Kate up a flight of stairs and down a long hallway Monday afternoon. The woman opened a set of French doors at the end of the hallway and stood back for Kate to enter. Kate stepped into a room completely decorated in gold. Mesmerized, she looked around. The walls were tufted gold-satin brocade. A pale, gold-and-white-striped, semicircular sofa sat in the middle of the room, with several small gold upholstered chairs and gleaming brass and glass tables. Overhead, a brass and crystal chandelier cast muted light onto the room.

"No, no, no, *chérie*," a heavily accented voice said. It reminded Kate of Zsa Zsa Gabor.

"Stand still, Jessica," Monica said.

"Kate! We're over here," Jessica said, calling out from behind an elaborate art-deco screen in the corner. "I'm so glad you came."

Kate set her handbag on a table and walked over to Jessica, who stood on a chair enveloped in a long white trumpet gown with a shimmery cape and silver and crystal embroidery.

A plump woman in a brightly colored duster was buttoning

the back of the gown. Kate saw Jessica's horrified expression in one of the tall mirrors that surrounded her on three sides. From every angle the attractive young woman was made to look short and dumpy in the elegant dress. She caught Kate's eye and gave her a pleading look. It was evident to Kate that the gown hadn't been designed for Jessica.

"This one will not do," the designer said. "I did not realize you are so short. We will try another." She began undoing the buttons.

"I sent you her measurements," Monica said, leaning back to gauge the fit. Jessica's cousin Kristin was sitting on a nearby couch, just watching, her eyes on the sumptuous gown.

"Yes, yes, and I will make alterations when she decides which gown she wants. This is not the one. My other clients will be beautiful in this one," she said as if Jessica was somehow less than ideally put together. She turned to Monica. "On you it would be perfect, *non*? I will set it aside for you, Monique," she said, giving Monica's name a French pronunciation. Monica didn't correct her.

Jessica tried to wiggle out of the gown.

"*Faire attention*," the woman snapped.

Kate held out her hand to help steady Jessica.

"Thank you," Jessica said, taking her hand and holding on while she stepped out of the gown. She started to get down off the chair, but Monica instructed her to stay put.

"Good afternoon, Kate," Monica said coolly. She sized Kate up, and Kate reflexively reached up to smooth her hair. "Jessica said she'd invited you to come see the dresses. You're in for a treat. This is Yvette d'Avril of New York."

The woman absently held out a hand to Kate. Kate shook it.

"It's very nice to meet you," Kate said, pasting a smile onto her face.

"Yvette brought her latest designs for Jessica to try on. We're most fortunate," Monica said, smiling as the designer turned away from Kate.

"I have not unveiled these designs to the public yet. You are the first to see them. I handpicked them for your daughter, Monica."

"Stepdaughter," Monica corrected.

"But, of course, that is what I meant. You are too young to have such a grown-up daughter." Yvette carefully packed the gown away, then zipped open another long clothing bag. Layers of embroidered chiffon spilled out as she lifted the gown from the bag. Kate leaned in to get a better look. The fabric was beautiful.

"This is very traditional," Yvette said as she held it up. "But I think it might be"—she cast a dismissive glance at Jessica— "a better fit."

Yvette and Kate helped Jessica put on the gown. It draped below her feet by at least six inches. The gown had a beaded empire bodice, and the skirt belled out from above the waist, hiding Jessica's petite figure completely. Again, she looked dumpy.

"That's beautiful," Kristin said, affecting a model's stance.

Yvette smiled at Kristin. "You would look stunning in all of my creations," she said.

Kristin blushed, then glanced at herself in the mirror.

The designer turned to Jessica. "Not to worry. You have a problem figure, *chérie*, but I have more beautiful gowns." She reached for another gown.

The fabric shimmered silver. A deep-cut bodice gave way to a long fitted dress with deep slits up the front and sides, revealing a silken underskirt. Translucent pewter organza flared out from the slits. The dress was stunning and would have looked gorgeous on someone tall and thin.

"Surely that's not a wedding dress," Jessica said, shaking her head and holding out her hands to ward off the gown.

"White is not so important these days, *chérie*. Women are daring to wear gowns that make them beautiful."

"I think I would really prefer something more traditional," Jessica said, biting her lip.

Yvette rolled her eyes and turned to Monica. "You would be fabulous in this creation. I designed it with you in mind."

Kate doubted that was true, but Monica seemed impressed.

"It'd make an awesome bridesmaid's dress," Kristin said, getting up to touch the shimmery fabric.

"We already picked the bridesmaids' dresses." Jessica shook her head. "My colors are pink and green, not silver."

"This is pewter, not silver. That is a big difference," Yvette said, accenting her words.

"I want to get married in white," Jessica said, crossing her arms over her chest.

"Then set that one aside," Monica said. "I'll try it on later."

"*Bon* . . . I have one more. I saved the *pièce de résistance* for last," Yvette declared as she reached for the final garment bag. She unzipped it to reveal a strapless silk taffeta dress with a dropped waist.

When Jessica put it on, the bouffant balloon skirt came to the top of her knees. The bodice was covered in delicate Chantilly lace with gold threads.

"That's more like it," Monica said, nodding. "That suits you."

Jessica stared in the mirror with dismay. "But Monica, I look like a little girl, not a bride." She brushed the poufed skirt, and it bounced back. "It's awful."

Monica sighed and put her hands on her hips. "You're running out of options, Jessica. Yvette was kind enough to come all the way here. The least you could do is try."

"*Amie*, you look like a celebrity, like that other Jessica, or Reese Witherspoon, *non*?" Yvette looked at Monica, then Kate for confirmation.

"No. I look like a . . . a puffy marshmallow," Jessica said.

Kristin snorted, then quickly covered her mouth as if to hide her gaffe. Jessica started wiggling out of the dress, and Kate stepped forward to help.

"Your designs are exquisite," Kate said, trying to encourage not only the designer but also Monica. Though she personally didn't love the styles, the fabrics were fabulous, and the designs, no doubt, very chic.

"Thank you." Yvette seemed to soak up the praise.

"Obviously, you cater to an elite clientele with tall, slender figures like Monica. It would be a shame to have to modify the lovely gowns from their original design."

Yvette smiled as she slipped the last gown back on its hanger.

"Do you have anything else in your studio that might work for Jessica?" Monica asked, holding her chin in her hand. "The wedding is scheduled for early November."

"*Quoi*? I cannot design a dress for *la petite jeune fille* in so short a time. *C'est impossible*."

"It's all right, Monica," Jessica said quickly. "Thank you so much, Yvette, for coming here and bringing these dresses. They really are beautiful. I know I'm hard to fit . . . I can just go down to Chattanooga and find a dress."

Yvette's head reared back. "You would buy a wedding dress off a rack?" She turned to Monica. "This is a calamity, *mon amie*. For you, I will try to create a dress in time, but I must have the girl come to New York."

"I can't," Jessica said. "I promised to substitute teach for the elementary school. I can't leave."

"This is more important than a part-time job," Monica said. She pulled a small leather datebook out of the purse at her feet. "Almost two hundred fifty guests are coming to see you get married, including some of your father's most influential friends. You can't get married in just any old dress. You have an image to uphold." She flipped through the pages of her date-book and turned to Yvette. "Would next week work for you?"

"I gave my word, Monica. I'm sorry," Jessica interrupted.

Monica sighed deeply. "I know you've had a tiring morn-ing, Yvette. Let me show you to your room so you can rest before dinner."

"*Très bien*. Do not forget to try on the two dresses we set aside for you. The pewter one would be stunning for the mother of the bride."

Monica winced. "Yes, I'll do that later." She turned to Jessica with a warning frown. "I'll be right back."

After the women left the room, Jessica plopped down next to Kristin on the couch in her slip and high heels and leaned her elbows on her knees, looking forlorn. Kate sat in a chair across from her.

"You're so lucky," Kristin said. "I can't believe you'd pass up a chance at a designer gown, especially since you don't even have to pay for it."

"I know . . . They really were beautiful, but they weren't for me."

Kristin nodded. "Monica wasn't really making it any easier, I guess."

"She was trying to help." Jessica sighed. "But I'm doing the best I can. I don't know what to do." She sat up straight and turned toward her cousin. "Is there any chance you'd want to go shopping with me for a dress?"

"No way." Kristin waved her hands in front of her face. "I don't want to get in Monica's bad graces." She laughed, but Jessica looked crushed.

"Look, I'll help you if you really need it," Kristin added quickly. She shook her head, and the expression on her face indicated that she wasn't thrilled about the chore. "I have to run, but give me a call later. We'll figure something out." She pushed herself up, sauntered across the carpeted floor, and walked out into the hallway without stopping to say good-bye.

Kate watched Jessica's cousin leave. Kristin didn't seem to be very supportive of Jessica. In fact, she seemed to be siding with Monica.

"Is it just me?" Jessica said, peering up at Kate. "Am I crazy? I didn't like any of the dresses, but they both acted like I was out of my mind."

"I suspect the gowns would create a stir at a New York fashion show, but they aren't designed for the average woman," Kate said.

"That's it. I'm too ordinary. I wish I weren't, so I could

please Monica, but I can't help it. I don't want to get married in a dress I detest." She looked up at Kate. "I don't know what to do."

"I'm sure you'll find a lovely dress, maybe in Chattanooga. No matter what you wear, you'll be a beautiful bride."

"Thanks," Jessica said, leaning her head back against the couch cushion. "I appreciate your being here."

Monica came back into the room silently, barely glancing at Kate before she stopped in front of Jessica. Her lips were pressed together, and her cheeks were pink. "I do my best, but I can't seem to please you," Monica said as if Kate wasn't even in the room.

It was the first real emotion Kate had seen from the step-mother, and even though she felt like an intruder, she didn't move. "You don't seem to care about your father and his feelings. He told me once that he promised your mother he'd give you a dream wedding when you got married." She shook her head.

"But I—"

"You're throwing your life away on a man who will never amount to anything, but your father is trying to overlook that and accept your decision because he wants you to be happy." Monica took a step closer to the couch, and Kate tried to suppress the chill she felt in her spine. "You've wasted your inheritance, and now you're rejecting your father's generosity." Monica's hands balled into tight fists. "How can you be so ungrateful?"

Jessica's head drew back, almost as if she'd been slapped. She blinked back tears. "I'm not, and I did not waste that money. I don't know what happened to it, but someone must have taken it." She looked at Monica with pursed lips.

"It was probably that man you're going to marry. All he's ever been after is your money."

Jessica opened her mouth to respond, but no sound came out.

"Your father checked his background, you know. Did he tell you Trace got fired from a job at a bank after some money disappeared?"

Jessica pushed herself up to her feet, and leaned in toward Monica. "I don't believe you. Trace isn't a thief. I know I can't convince you of that, but I trust him." She took a deep breath as tears welled up in her eyes. "Look, I really appreciate all you and Daddy are doing, but Trace and I *are* getting married, and we just want a simple wedding. We don't want all the fancy trappings."

"If you insist on going through with this wedding, we'll do it the right way. Just don't disappoint your father more than you already have." Monica sighed. "This dress fiasco is costing me ten thousand dollars." She gave Jessica a slightly rueful look and shook her head. "I'm buying an expensive gown to appease Yvette and make it worth her while coming down here, and you still don't have a wedding dress."

She turned to Kate. "You're the one who's supposed to be counseling her. Maybe you can talk some sense into her. I give up."

Jessica looked at Kate, her eyes wide. Kate gave her a little nod, hoping to convey encouragement, even though her mind was still reeling about Monica's bombshell concerning

Trace's background. Trace seemed sincere, and he gave all the right answers at the counseling sessions, but Kate knew people weren't always what they appeared to be.

Kate didn't know what to believe, but she intended to find out the truth about Jessica's fiancé.

Chapter Six

As Kate left Gentian Hill Manor, she couldn't get Monica's charge against Trace out of her mind. Anyone could get fired or laid off from a job. Even if he had been fired, that didn't prove anything unless he'd been charged with a crime. But if he had gotten away with embezzling funds once, perhaps he'd done it twice. No matter what had really happened, Gordon and Monica believed the worst, which didn't bode well for their future relationship with Trace or Jessica. Jessica believed in Trace, but doubts could creep in so easily.

She drove down the hill past her house and went on to the library. The Internet was the best place to start looking.

When Kate entered the library, she spotted Livvy at the front counter checking out books. Livvy looked up and waved as Kate passed her and went up the stairs. School was out for the day, and teenagers sat at most of the computer terminals, but Kate found one empty spot. She logged on to the Internet and typed the name "Trace Jackson" into the search engine. Pages and pages of references came up.

As she scanned through the search results, she found sites that contained the words separately but not together as a full name. Then there was a site dedicated to a former band called Jackson Trace. That wasn't it either. Several pages down, she found a list of old references to a bank fiasco in newspaper archives. Kate clicked on the first link that took her to a news article from a Richmond, Virginia, newspaper three years prior.

Federal Reserve Board investigates Lynchburg Branch of Appomattox Commercial Bank Corp.

Johnson Wholesale Tools, Inc., and Bardol Tool and Die shorted $10,000. Bank employee Trace Jackson admits encoding error caused funds shortage. Bank cannot account for the missing funds.

According to the paper, there had been an encoding error, and no theft was mentioned. Kate had no idea what an encoding error was. Had Trace made an entry error—perhaps accidentally redirecting funds to the wrong account—or had he stolen bank funds? And if the funds had been redirected to another account, why couldn't the bank simply have retrieved them?

Kate opened another Internet window and did a Google search for "encoding error." She discovered that encoding errors were common in banks, but they were usually resolved within a couple of weeks. They occurred when a bank employee mistyped a routing number on a check. The Web site showed that, typically, encoding errors were easily traced. But if that was the case, how could the ten thousand dollars have gone missing?

Kate returned to her original search and found several more articles on the fiasco. Another bank employee had been questioned about the error, but when Kate did a search for the man—Art Franklin—no new information resulted.

The final article she found about the incident stated that Trace Jackson had been relieved of his job and had left under a cloud of suspicion. Though he'd never been charged or accused of a crime, he'd never been cleared, either, and the money still seemed to be missing.

Kate sat back and stared at the computer screen, thinking through all she knew about Trace Jackson. At their first counseling session, Jessica said she'd met Trace three years ago. She'd said it was love at first sight.

He knew his way around a computer and the inner workings of bank transactions. He had a degree in computer science. No doubt he knew how to access Jessica's trust fund. But that didn't mean he did it, and if he did, what did he do with the money?

Kate printed out the most complete article she could find, put it in her handbag, and walked down the stairs toward the exit. As she strode out of the library, she thought through her research. There was still so much she needed to learn about Trace Jackson.

KATE STEPPED OUT of the pharmacy the next afternoon, and as she started to open her car door, she heard a whinny and glanced down the street toward the creek. Two horses came into view along the creek path. One of the riders waved, and Kate recognized Jessica. She waved back. Jessica turned her horse and started ambling up the street toward her. A moment later, the second horse followed, ridden by Brian Levy.

Jessica pulled her horse to a stop next to Kate. Kate felt intimidated by its huge size, but the majestic white horse looked down at her, with its large, lustrous dark eyes showing more curiosity than challenge. Jessica sat astride an English saddle and looked like a member of the English gentry in her black riding apparel and white ruffled blouse. Her long blonde hair spilled out beneath her helmet. She reached out and patted the horse's neck.

"Good girl," she said. "She's very gentle."

The horse nickered softly. Kate reached up and gently smoothed its velvety soft nose. It rubbed against her hand, and Kate fell in love with the beautiful beast.

Brian struck quite a contrast in jeans and a red plaid shirt cut in western fashion. He rode western saddle but wore a helmet instead of a cowboy hat. Ashland Street dead-ended at the creek, so there wasn't any traffic for the horses to negotiate.

"I'm glad I ran into you," Jessica said. "I told Flora about the wedding-dress debacle, and she had an idea. She took my mother's things up to the attic when Monica moved in, and she thinks Mama's old wedding dress might be up there somewhere. She said she'd come over and help me sort through Mama's things tomorrow morning, and she invited you to come too."

"Oh?" Kate tilted her head and watched Jessica.

Jessica shrugged. "She said you two really hit it off. I'd love for you to be there. Could you come?"

Kate had planned to spend the day in her studio designing

stained-glass pieces for her holiday collection, but she supposed she could take a little time, especially after Flora's veiled remarks at the shower. "I can come for a while. What time?"

"Ten thirty? Can you stay and have some lunch afterward?"

"I'd be delighted."

Kate's eyes met Brian's.

"Excuse my bad manners," Jessica said. "Did you meet Brian Saturday at the shower?"

"We weren't formally introduced. I'm Kate Hanlon," she said, holding out her hand.

"Pleased to meet you," Brian said. "I had a chance to talk to your husband for a few minutes the other day. He said you moved here from Texas. I live in New Mexico, near Ruidoso."

"That's a beautiful part of the country." Kate noticed mud on his riding boots, but other than that, he was well put together. "So what brings you to Copper Mill, Brian?"

"A mix of business and pleasure." His eyes went to Jessica, but she was half turned away from him and didn't see. Kate saw it, though, and she could tell his interest was more than platonic. "Gordon and I have business to discuss, but this is off-season for me at the ranch, so coming here gives me a chance to catch up on old friendships too."

Jessica glanced back over her shoulder and gave her companion an affectionate smile. "Brian taught me to ride when I was barely walking."

"And she took to it like she was born in the saddle. All her trophies prove that."

Jessica dipped her head and blushed.

"She's modest, but she was a contender for the Olympic

team," Brian said, his tone filled with pride. "She's taken lots of trophies in dressage, but you should see her jump. She's amazing."

"Brian." Jessica frowned. "All that is behind me. I'm not competing anymore."

"Just because you're getting married?" Brian sighed. "Never mind. None of my business, I guess." He raised an eyebrow and turned back to Kate.

"It was nice meeting you," he said to Kate and nudged his horse into motion. "I'll wait for you down by the creek," he called to Jessica, then clicked the reins and slowly moseyed away.

Jessica watched him go, then turned back to Kate. "Don't mind him. He doesn't think I can be happy unless I'm on a horse."

"Does Trace ride?" Kate asked.

"Not yet. Four-wheeled ATVs are his choice of steed, but he's willing to learn. If he ever has time, that is." She reined to the right.

"Do you keep in touch with Brian much?" Kate asked. "When he's not here, I mean?"

Jessica cast her eyes to Brian, who was picking his way down the bank. "Here and there. Mostly he just talks to my father about horses, though."

Kate wasn't sure, but she thought she saw a hint of disappointment in Jessica's face.

Jessica looked back at Kate and offered her a smile. "I'd better go catch up with Brian before he wanders too far off. He doesn't have an ounce of patience. Never did. See you tonight."

Kate watched Jessica's horse amble down the street, then pull up beside Brian's. The two horses slowly walked downstream side by side. Brian and Jessica were looking at each other rather than the pathway, trusting the horses to navigate on their own. Kate had to admit they made a handsome pair, both horses and riders.

Brian had already been in town at least a week. How long could his business take? His timing seemed too propitious to be a coincidence. He might have come to discuss horses with Gordon, but Kate suspected that he'd stayed on because of Jessica. Was Gordon or Monica encouraging Brian to distract Jessica with reminders of her past?

Kate shook her head. She was imagining things. But Brian *had* come into town just around the time Jessica discovered that her trust fund had been drained. How did he fit into this puzzle?

All Kate knew for sure was that someone had hundreds of thousands of reasons to steal the money from Jessica's trust fund.

Chapter Seven

I made my budget," Jessica said quietly. "It's not very complete, I'm afraid."

Jessica, Trace, Paul, and Kate were sitting in Paul's office at the church having their third premarital counseling session. Jessica held a computer printout.

"The trust paid all my expenses from the time I went away to boarding school. I had a monthly allowance, so I had to budget that, I suppose, but it was pretty generous. I just paid for personal things, like snacks and entertainment, but I didn't keep track of my expenditures. So making a list was a bit of a challenge." She held the paper out to Paul.

"I know how much Trace pays in rent, and I made up a grocery list of basics that I thought we'd need and then went to the store and priced them. I was shocked at how much groceries cost. Then there's household utilities and gas and maintenance for our cars, as well as insurance and medical expenses."

Kate smiled. Jessica had put more thought into this than she had expected.

"By the time we pay our bills, there's nothing left for personal care or vacations or even cable TV and Internet, let alone for savings or emergencies." Jessica's shoulders slumped. She looked defeated before she even started. Kate's heart went out to the younger woman.

"We're not that bad off," Trace said, reaching over to squeeze his fiancée's hand. Then he leaned forward, his elbows on his knees. "I've budgeted for years, so I know how to stretch a dollar." He unfolded his list. "I admit I ate pretty simply in college. Mainly PBJs and tomato soup and lots of cold cereal, but I figure Jessica and I can brown bag our lunches for a while and be fine."

He looked at Paul, then down at his list. "My apartment is small, but it'll do until we get on our feet. I included tithing to church and a small monthly donation to the Special Olympics. That's my favorite charity. I've been supporting it for years." He looked over at Jessica. "We'll be tight for a while, but we'll make it."

"Jessica, I've heard you say that you want pets. Did you factor that into your budget?" Paul asked.

"We can't afford it. In fact, I don't know what I'll do with my horse. Monica told me I need to pay to board it at the stable. She said I'm an adult now, and I have to pay my own way. I can't bear the thought of selling her, but I may have to."

Trace frowned. "Seems like she could have waited to dump that on you."

"I have to face it sooner or later. Like Monica said, I have to pay my own way. I'm broke, and I can't expect Daddy to bail me out." Jessica shrugged. "At least Monica's being honest."

Kate looked from Jessica to Trace, sensing the tension

between them. Paul shot her a look indicating he noticed it too.

"How did you do on the other part of last week's assignment —talking about your differences and expectations?" Paul asked.

Jessica and Trace looked at each other. Trace looked away.

"We did great on some parts. We both want the Lord to be central in our marriage," Jessica said. "We didn't do so well talking about our pasts, though." She looked at Kate. "I brought up what Monica said, but he won't discuss it."

Trace shuffled his feet. "There's nothing to talk about."

"There's plenty to talk about," Jessica said, her voice rising a little. "You were accused of taking money. I know you'd never do that, but I want my father and Monica to believe in you too. Why won't you defend yourself and tell us what happened?"

Trace looked down at the floor and shook his head. "Can't you just trust me?"

"I do. I trust you. But Daddy wants to protect me. Can't you see that?"

"That about says it all, doesn't it?" He ran his hands through his hair and looked over at his fiancée. "I don't want to come between you and your father, but he's trying to pull us apart. He's the one pushing you to choose between us."

Jessica didn't say a word but just stared at Trace. Kate looked at Paul.

Paul leaned forward, looking first at Trace, then at Jessica. He usually led couples through premarital counseling with a gentle touch, allowing them to explore their relationship and make discoveries together. But he could also be firm, and Kate sensed one of those moments coming. Marriage was too important to leave any misconceptions alone.

"You two are about to commit to the closest human relationship that life offers. There should be no secrets or subjects that you keep from each other. A wife needs to trust that her husband loves her above any other person and will protect her with his life, if necessary. A husband needs to trust that his wife respects him as a man of God and as a husband and loves him above all others. That's straight out of Ephesians 5:33. It says, 'Each one of you also must love his wife as he loves himself, and the wife must respect her husband.'"

Paul sat back in his chair. "If you can make this a firm commitment to each other now before you marry, you'll get a head start on working through the problems that may come along."

Jessica looked at Trace, her eyes begging him to trust her with whatever he was holding back. Trace pursed his lips, a stoic expression on his face, and looked straight ahead. Paul gave Kate a look of unease. Her eyes echoed his concern. She believed that Trace and Jessica loved each other, but they had some serious issues to overcome. She prayed they could either work through them before the wedding or have the wisdom to step back and reevaluate their relationship.

KATE FELT A LITTLE STRANGE about being with Jessica when she opened her mother's trunks, but she was glad to be invited to witness the event. She thought of all the fun and confidences she'd shared with her daughters as they matured into young women. Jessica was missing that special time with her mother, especially as she planned her wedding. Kate had seen her wistful expression more than once as they'd talked. More than that, though, Kate hoped she'd get a chance to talk to Flora about what was really going on.

As before, Monica's housekeeper, Helen, let Kate into the mansion. Monica was nowhere to be seen, but Jessica and Flora were visiting in the living room, waiting for her. Jessica jumped up, a glow of excitement on her face, and gave Kate a hug.

"Thanks for coming. I can't wait to see what's in those trunks. I didn't even know about them until last week, or I'd have been into them a long time ago."

"They were put up so long ago, I had completely forgotten about them," Flora said, rubbing her hip as she pushed herself to her feet.

Kate wondered how Flora could have forgotten a detail as important as an heirloom wedding dress, but she shrugged off the thought.

"I don't even know what all's in them," Jessica said, "but it's worth a look, isn't it? Wouldn't it be amazing if my mother's dress really was in one of those trunks?" Jessica interlaced her hands over her heart and did a little jump.

"Thanks for inviting me to come today. I'm a sucker for a mystery! I'm almost as excited as you to learn what your mother stored away."

Jessica took Kate's arm. "Well, let's get to it! Lead the way, Flora."

"Will do, Miss Jessica. My old bones don't move so easily these days, so let's take the elevator."

Kate and Jessica followed Flora slowly out of the room, then turned down the hallway and made their way to an elevator near the back of the house. Kate was surprised how large the elevator was. They got in, and Jessica pushed the button for the third floor. The elevator groaned loudly as it rose.

"This lift goes to the attic," Flora said. "They use it to move furniture and such into storage, but I doubt it's used much anymore. Monica got rid of most of everything."

"You know this house well," Kate said, smiling at Flora.

"Oh yes." Flora reached out and touched the wall to steady herself as the elevator shuddered. "I worked here for most of my life, caring for Mrs. Amelia, and then Miss Jessica. This old place is as familiar as my own home."

Kate watched Flora. There was a sadness in her eyes as she talked about the old days. Kate suspected that Flora and her husband probably knew much more about what had gone on in the house than anyone.

"So, Kate, umm . . . have you had any luck? With the trust fund?" Jessica's face was almost pleading.

Kate shook her head. "But I'm looking into a few leads," she said, trying to keep her voice hopeful. She let her eyes gaze downward. Kate wasn't ready to tell Jessica about her research into Trace's background. She just wasn't sure how the young woman would feel if she learned that Kate was investigating her fiancé. Would she feel betrayed? When Kate lifted her eyes, she noticed Flora watching her.

"Thank you, Kate." Jessica said. "I wish money wasn't such a big issue with my family. I mean, I understand that money's important, but my family seems so fixated on it. And now that Monica is hinting that Trace isn't trustworthy, well . . . I just hope we can prove her wrong."

Kate noted that Jessica didn't mention proving her father wrong, even though Monica had said that Gordon was the one looking into Trace's background. Did Monica put Gordon up to investigating Trace? Or perhaps Jessica just didn't want to think about her own father's doubts about her fiancé. Kate knew that Gordon adored his daughter. Still, he had good reason to be suspicious of Trace, and to make matters worse, he was torn between two women. A perilous place for the poor man.

"I knew you'd be good for my Jessica," Flora said to Kate as the elevator stopped. "She needs an ally around here."

Kate glanced at Flora and smiled. She prayed she could be the ally Jessica needed. On the other hand, she was worried that so far her investigation had led nowhere.

The elevator door slid open, and they stepped into the attic. It took Kate a moment to adjust to the dim light. Dust motes hung in the air, disturbed by the movement of the elevator doors and made visible by the filtered light that seeped through the dingy attic dormer windows. Flora flipped a switch, and a row of lights on the ceiling flickered to life. A jumble of boxes and odd furniture occupied one side of the cavernous room. Flora started shuffling to the far end of the long room, stirring up more dust.

"Grab two chairs and bring them along," Flora called behind her. "You don't want to sit on the floor over here. It's much too dusty."

Kate picked up a chair and carried it to the end of the row, dodging piles of boxes and furniture covered in sheets. Flora beckoned to her around a corner and turned on another overhead light.

"I think the trunks might be over this way. Go ahead and put the chairs there, then sit down," she told Kate and Jessica.

On Kate's left, large sheets covered what looked like two long caskets.

"Let me help you," Kate said, going over to pick up one end of each sheet. She helped Flora fold the sheets inward, trapping the dust. Beneath were beautifully carved mahogany chests.

"Oh!" Jessica clapped her hands together, then came over and passed her hand over the lovely wood. "I remember these. They belonged to my grandmother." She turned and hugged Flora.

"Monica wanted all this to be thrown away, but I packed it all up and moved everything up here until you were old enough to appreciate it. I don't know which trunk the dress would be in, though." The elderly woman stepped back and surveyed the trunks, then she crouched down, reached behind one of them, and felt along the back side.

"Aha!" she said as she struggled with what sounded like a piece of tape. A moment later she straightened up and handed Jessica a key, then she went over and lowered herself into a nearby rocking chair. "Kate, maybe you could help her. I think some of the contents may be brittle by now."

"All right." Kate resisted the urge to rub her hands together in anticipation of what she might learn from these treasures. There *had* to be some clue in all this. She knew that one could tell a lot about people by their discarded things, and this attic was chock-full of them.

Jessica bent down to unlock one of the chests. Flora was leaning back, hands folded in her lap, her eyes fixed on Jessica. Jessica raised a lid to reveal what looked like a trunk filled with tissue paper. She lifted something out and began unwrapping it.

"Oh, I remember this," she exclaimed. She held up a

dainty porcelain cup covered with roses. She set it aside with great care, then took out another object wrapped in tissue. "Is the whole set here?"

"There was a full service for twelve," Flora said. "It's probably all still there."

"How wonderful! I can have a tea party. Maybe I could have one before the wedding, when my friends and Trace's family get here. Remember Mama's tea parties, Flora?"

"Indeed I do. I taught her how to make scones that would melt in your mouth."

"Can you show *me*?" Jessica asked.

"I'd be happy to. You can come too, Kate."

"Oh, thank you. I'd love to. I have a wonderful collection of teapots, and I put on tea parties for our church ladies once in a while. I try to be authentic, but I've never learned how to make a proper English tea."

Flora nodded once. "Good. It's settled, then. You and Jessica come to my cottage tomorrow afternoon. We'll have English tea with all the dainties."

Kate watched the former housekeeper. She felt honored to be included in all these activities, but what was Flora up to? Had she really forgotten that Amelia's trunks were stored up in the attic? And why had she spoken so mysteriously with Kate at the shower? She had said they needed to talk. About what?

Kate pulled her chair over near Flora and sat down, working hard at observing the woman without acting too obvious about her curiosity.

Kate also watched Jessica as she lifted piles of linens out of the trunk: fine lace tablecloths, napkins, crocheted doilies, and embroidered dresser scarves. Jessica handled each piece with care, examining each heirloom with rapt attention, then smoothing it with her hand as she set it aside. Her expression seemed more somber than joyful. These treasures came from her mother and surely evoked strong memories, but Kate hoped the beauty of her memories outweighed the renewed sense of loss.

While Jessica continued unpacking the trunk, Flora motioned for Kate to lean in closer, so she edged a little more to the left.

"Something isn't right with that new gardener at the estate," Flora said under her breath. "The one Monica hired. If I were looking for missing money, that's where I'd start."

Kate stared at Flora and exhaled, realizing this must be what Flora had wanted to talk about. Still, Kate wasn't sure what to make of the former housekeeper's advice, and she couldn't interpret the strange expression on her face. Flora knew the family so well. Could she also know about their financial interests? Or did Flora have her own reasons for directing Kate's investigation toward Monica's employee?

The first trunk seemed to hold no hint of wedding finery, so Jessica moved to the second and carefully worked the lock. Inside, she uncovered embroidered and lacy linen handkerchiefs, a rectangular celluloid box decorated with roses, and another box that held several pairs of gloves—a pair of short lace gloves; sheer gloves without fingers, but ruffled at the wrists; and pale pink kid leather gloves.

Next, Jessica opened a white dress box full of baby clothes. She looked up at Flora with luminous eyes. "These were mine, weren't they?"

Flora just grinned.

Jessica held up a soft pink cotton toddler's dress with white lace and puffy sleeves. "No wonder I love pink," she said. Then she took out a yellow outfit.

"You wore that on your first Easter. You looked like a little buttercup."

Jessica held the little dress against her heart and stared at Flora.

"You used to call me Buttercup. Is that why?"

Flora chuckled. "You went for the buttercups from the moment you could toddle along in the garden. You would pick them, then hold them to your nose and sniff. The pollen would get on your nose, and then you would sneeze and the force of it would knock you over. You'd look so startled sitting there with your eyes all big and round. Your mother would snatch you up and kiss you on the neck, and you'd giggle and forget about your spill until the next time. That's when I started calling you Buttercup."

Jessica got up and gave Flora another hug.

"Oh, now," Flora sputtered, but she looked pleased. "Get on with looking through those trunks. It's stuffy up here."

Kate watched the two, touched to witness the long-standing camaraderie between them. Flora obviously loved Jessica.

"All right." Jessica obediently leaned over the trunk and pulled out several sheets of tissue.

She gasped. Her hands flew to her mouth. "Oh, Flora. Oh!" She reached in and reverently lifted out a cloud of pure white and held it up. It fell open in soft folds of fabric. "Mama's wedding dress. Kate, look." She eyed it silently for a long moment. "I wonder if it fits me."

She stood up, letting the heavy skirt cascade to its full length. Out of the corner of her eye, Kate saw something fall out of the folds of the skirt. Jessica was too excited to notice the small tap as it hit the dusty wooden floor, but Kate saw Flora eyeing the small yellowed envelope.

"Can you help me?" Jessica asked.

Kate and Flora turned their attention back to the girl and helped fluff out the yards and yards of satin skirt. The dress had a long fitted bodice that came down to a dropped waistline. Thin straps of delicate embroidered roses were attached to the princess neckline and edged the seam separating the torso from the full skirt. Fine tulle netting overlaid the skirt. Jessica held the bodice up to her, and Kate stepped away, letting the skirt fall gently against the girl. Kate glanced over to where the envelope had fallen. It was gone.

The elevator dinged. The door opened, and footsteps advanced toward them. A moment later, Monica appeared around the corner.

"There you are." She waved a hand around her head as if pushing away cobwebs. "I've been looking all over for you." She was dressed for riding. All she lacked was a helmet and riding crop. "What in the world?" She took in the scene. "Oh, you found your mother's trunks." She sighed. "I hope you're not too disappointed. I told Florence you wouldn't want that old stuff."

Kate noted how Monica called Flora by her formal name. She almost felt sorry for Monica; it seemed as if she was being purposefully withdrawn. Was there a softer woman behind all that poise?

She came closer, squinting against the dim light. "Oh my.

Was that your grandmother's wedding dress? It looks like it belongs in a museum."

"It was my mother's," Jessica said, raising her chin. "And I think I'm going to wear it in my wedding."

"Oh." Monica swallowed. "But the dress is old and dingy. It's terribly out of style and probably falling apart." She sighed. "I'd rather buy you a new dress. Surely we can find something, even if it is short notice."

"No, thanks, Monica. If it fits me, this is what I want to wear."

Monica stiffened and looked at Kate and Flora. "We'll talk about this later," she said.

Jessica slightly shook her head, then looked up at Monica and gave her a strained smile. "Are you going to join us for lunch?"

"No. I have a tennis match, and I need to change or I'll be late." She turned around and left, her riding boots clicking on the floor as she marched to the elevator. As she walked away, Kate realized she hadn't mentioned why she'd been looking for Jessica.

Chapter Eight

K ate noticed subtle hints of yellow and gold in the surrounding landscape as she drove west of town Thursday afternoon. She was looking for Queen Anne Lane, a fitting address for the residence of an English lady.

She almost missed it. Barely visible beyond a large mountain ash, she spotted a white mailbox with lacy flowers painted on the side atop a white post. Kate turned into a narrow tree-lined drive. The trees gave way to a clearing.

A riot of color surrounded a quaint brick cottage. A long sloping tiled roof reached nearly to the ground on one side and had three dormers across the upper story. Ivy grew up the large stone chimney, and green shutters set off the small-paned windows across the front of the house. Bright red roses grew up the sides and covered an arched entrance. Kate felt as if she'd stepped into a fairy tale when she walked into the yard, but then she saw two small satellite dishes on the roof and knew she was in the twenty-first century.

"Hello, Kate."

Kate gasped and looked into the bushes, where the voice had come from.

"Bertie." Kate put her hand to her heart. The retired gardener was crouched down on the ground, digging at the root of a rosebush. "I didn't see you there."

"Didn't mean to scare you," he laughed, leaning back on his feet. "Just wanted to say welcome and go right on in. Flora's all excited that you're coming." He gave a wave and turned back to the rosebush. Kate continued up the path to the door.

"You're here!" Jessica bounded through the front door. "Isn't it gorgeous? The landscaping is mostly Bertie's work. I told him I want some of these plants for my yard." Her smile faltered. "That is when I get a yard. Come on in. Flora is just getting ready to make the scones."

Kate followed Jessica into the cool, dim interior. Just off the entry was the parlor, furnished with old-fashioned upholstered furniture. Past it, through an open doorway, Kate could see bookshelves and a desk. A computer sat on top of the desk. With two satellite dishes, the Ripples also must have had high-speed Internet. Quite a luxury for a retired housekeeper and gardener.

They went into a small dining room at the back of the house. An old-fashioned wood stove on a brick hearth occupied one corner. A counter and upper glass cabinets displaying English bone china separated the dining area from a modern kitchen with stainless-steel appliances. Kate leaned in to look at some Dresden figurines on a whatnot shelf. The detail on a curtsying lady was amazing. Next to her, a gent was bowing. His striped pants matched her striped underskirt.

"Welcome." Flora came out of a pantry wearing a ruffled

apron and carrying a large copper tin. She set it on the counter. "You're just in time. We're ready to make the scones. We'll make three kinds, so we each have a batch."

The long counter had enough room for each of them to mix their dough.

"The secret to great scones," Flora said as she handed out recipes, "is the same as flaky pie crust—handling the dough with a gentle touch. Kate, you make the cranberry with orange zest. Jessica, make the chocolate-chip scones, and I'll make the apricot with almonds."

Kate mixed the ingredients in her bowl and used the pastry blender to work the butter into the dry ingredients until she had a fine meal.

Flora came next to Kate. "Excellent. You handle that like a trained chef," Flora said. "You have the touch, I can tell."

"Thank you." Kate felt her cheeks flushing. "I love to bake and try new recipes."

"There's nothing as satisfying as turning something fine out of an oven." Flora said. She turned her attention to her bowl. "Now mix together your milk and sour cream—that's another part of the secret—and stir it in gently until the ingredients are just moistened. Don't overmix it. That's right," she said to Jessica as the young woman mixed her dough with a fork.

"Now we dump it out, thus." Flora turned her dough onto a lightly floured surface and barely kneaded it, then patted it into rounds and cut it into wedges.

Jessica and Kate did likewise, then they arranged the wedges on cookie sheets and slid the sheets into the hot oven while Flora set the timer. Kate felt comfortable with most of the techniques Flora was teaching, but she was happy for the refresher.

Flora washed her hands and put on a kettle of cold water to boil. "It's such a lovely day, I thought we'd take tea outdoors. Oh, there's Bertie." She waved through the kitchen window, beckoning for him to come inside.

"Oh good. Just like old times," Jessica said.

A moment later, Bertie stuck his head through the doorway.

"I'll be ready to serve tea in a few minutes," Flora said to her husband. "Come wash up and join us."

"Don't mind if I do." He stomped his feet on the porch mat and hit his hat against his pant leg, then came in.

"I can't tell you often enough how much I love your flowers, Bertie," Jessica said, smiling at the old gardener. "Some day, I'll come get some slips and starts from you."

"Your mother would love that, bless her soul." Bertie smiled, then frowned. "We saved as much of the garden as we could when that . . . that upstart Monica hired started ripping out all the roses. Anthony piled them in a heap to burn."

"Poor Bertie about had a heart attack," Flora added, "but we saved them and brought them here."

"Mind you, Anthony does fine work," Bertie said, putting his hands under the faucet. He rubbed them together under the water to wash the dirt away. "And it is Monica's garden now, after all. He's done a good job, but it doesn't look like our home anymore."

"I just don't like having someone like *that* hanging around Gentian Hill Manor," Flora said.

"'Someone like that'?" Kate asked. "What do you mean?"

"He's"—Flora put her hand up to her face to cover her

mouth, as if keeping Bertie and Jessica from hearing what she was about to say—"a gangster." Flora dropped her hand and pressed her lips together as if she'd said too much, then turned a bit red in the face. She looked at Bertie, who looked just as uncomfortable.

"A gangster?" Jessica said. She giggled. "No way, Flora."

"She just means it's a crime what he did to your mother's beautiful gardens," Bertie added quickly.

"But we managed to save some of it, didn't we Bertie?" Flora said, nodding. "Bertie moved the gazebo here piece by piece and put it back together. That's where we'll be having tea."

The kettle whistled, and Flora got busy steeping the tea. Kate thought the retired housekeeper looked relieved to end the conversation. The timer buzzed, and Jessica took the scones out of the oven. The rich, warm scent of fresh scones and sweet chocolate filled the air. They carried the tea, scones, and a variety of finger foods outside.

Kate lagged behind the others a bit, trying to get a second alone with Flora to ask her about the envelope from the trunk, but the older woman deftly picked up her pace and avoided her. Kate quickened her step to catch up. What was in that envelope, and why did Flora want to keep it hidden?

The gazebo was made of redwood and was draped with gauze curtains that were tied back with cords. Pots of minia- ture roses surrounded the gazebo. A small waterfall gurgled as it spilled over rocks into a little pond surrounded by ferns, silvery hostas, red and black variegated coleus, and bright flowering impatiens.

"Your yard is magnificent," Kate said, gazing around at the lush lawn and gardens.

"Bertie is a genius," Flora said, beaming with pride. "The yard was a bramble patch when we moved in. We lived in a caretaker's house at the estate until we retired, you know, and when we bought this little place, it had been empty for years. Luckily, Monica was intent on redoing everything at the big house, and Mr. Mackenzie told us to take whatever we wanted. So that's how we ended up with such beautiful furnishings. He said he didn't care what I did with them. That's when I set aside a few things for Jessica."

She smiled at Jessica, then turned to Kate. "Would you ask a blessing on our little feast?"

"I'd love to."

Kate bowed her head and thanked the Lord for the lovely food and for new friends, then Flora passed her a plate of finger sandwiches. She took two. They'd been cut into hearts with a cookie cutter. She put a scone on her plate and filled it with clotted cream and lemon curd and a dab of homemade strawberry jam.

"The roses are fabulous," Kate said, gesturing to a lush green bush behind Jessica. "I didn't know they'd keep blooming so well this late."

"They'll still be blooming in a month if we don't get a hard freeze," Bertie said. "The secret is deadheading and pruning. I keep on top of them all summer, and they just keep blooming."

"Jessica described her mother's gardens to me," Kate went on, "but seeing what you've done here, I can begin to imagine how beautiful it was. It must have taken years for Anthony to make all those changes to the grounds."

"Oh no. It's only been in the past few months," Flora said, spreading a thin layer of butter across a strawberry scone. "He brought in a bunch of young men. Looked like hoodlums to me. They laughed and joked in Italian, even though they're from out east. I asked Anthony who they all were, and he told me they were part of 'the family.'" It sounded as though Flora was trying to imitate a New Jersey accent. "That's what they call the mob, you know," she said, nodding sagely.

Kate nearly choked on a bite of scone at the bizarre insinuation, and Jessica coughed into her napkin. Kate noticed her eyes were watering. Whether from mirth or dismay, she couldn't tell.

One thing was for sure: Flora had quite an imagination. Still, Anthony was spending a lot of time at the estate and could have fairly easy access to the Mackenzies' private information. Kate doubted he had any connection to the mafia, but he could easily snoop around and glean information. Had *he* discovered a way to access Jessica's trust fund?

A BRIGHT RED CONVERTIBLE sped up the road behind Kate Friday afternoon, following her as she turned into the Mackenzie driveway.

The early afternoon sun glinted off the hood, so she couldn't see the driver in her rearview mirror. The car slowed behind her, then when Kate reached the large circle drive in front of the mansion, it veered off to the right. She caught a glimpse of Jessica's cousin Kristin before the convertible disappeared around the side of the house. Then another car pulled into the driveway and parked next to Kate's car, and a moment later a middle-aged woman got out.

"Is this the Mackenzie place?" she asked, taking in the enormous house in front of her.

"Yes. You must be the seamstress. I'm Kate Hanlon, a friend of the bride."

The woman introduced herself as Mrs. Todd, then got a small case out of the car. They went to the door together, and the housekeeper led them to the sitting room where Jessica had tried on designer dresses earlier that week.

Before they reached the end of the hallway, Kate could tell that Kristin had found Jessica, because she could hear them arguing.

"I can't believe you'd just go into my jewelry case and take my watch without even asking me," Jessica said.

"I was just borrowing it," Kristin said, her voice low and even. "I was going to bring it back. You never wear it anyway. You don't even like red."

Kate and Mrs. Todd stepped inside the room, but Jessica and Kristin didn't even seem to notice.

"It was a gift. It's special to me because of that." Jessica blew out a breath. "And I never said I don't like red."

"Are you kidding? Everything you wear is pastel."

"That doesn't make it right to take my things. You need to ask first, Kristin." Jessica's face was flushed, and her normally sweet voice sounded a little strained.

"Okay. Fine." Kristin held up her hands in defeat. "I'm sorry. I should have asked."

Jessica's face relaxed a bit.

"Can I borrow your new jacket?" Kristin continued.

Jessica's eyes narrowed and then widened in surprise. "Is

that *my* new jacket you're wearing?" She reached out and touched the light gray wool. "I haven't even worn it yet!"

"I'm breaking it in for you." Kristin pulled at the lapels. "You have to admit, it looks good on me."

Jessica put her hands on her hips. Kristin threw up her hands.

"Okay, okay. I'll put it back. It's no big deal. You didn't even miss it until I showed up wearing it." Kristin turned and saw Kate and the seamstress. "Looks like you've got company," she said.

Jessica turned toward them and smiled. "Hi, Kate ... Mrs. Todd. I'm so glad you could come. Kristin, Mrs. Todd is going to alter my wedding dress for me."

"You already found a dress?" Kristin blinked a few times. "How lucky." Her tone sounded doubtful.

"It's gorgeous. It was my mother's wedding dress."

Kristin plopped down on the couch. "This I gotta see."

Kate wondered again about the cousins' relationship. Livvy had mentioned that Kristin used to stay at the estate often. She still seemed to feel right at home there, and she obviously felt no compunction about taking Jessica's things. But borrowing a watch was different than taking money, wasn't it? Kate shook her head. Kristin definitely manipulated her cousin, but Jessica either didn't seem to notice or was remarkably forgiving. Maybe she was just used to her cousin's attitude.

Jessica opened a tall closet and took out the dress. Kate helped her put it on and fasten the thirty small buttons up the back. Fine embroidered netting billowed over the skirt.

Standing in front of the large mirrors, Jessica held out the skirt and twirled around, her eyes alight with happiness. The dress fit with room to spare. It only needed a few adjustments.

"You look like Glinda the Good Witch in *The Wizard of Oz*," Kristin said. "All you need is a magic wand."

Jessica glared at her cousin. Kate couldn't figure out what to make of that comment either.

"You're really going to wear that?" Kristin continued.

Jessica's face fell. Then she frowned. "Yes, I'm going to wear it."

"Oh." Kristin stood up and walked toward her cousin. She lifted a section of the delicate netting and examined it, then let it fall. "Well, maybe if you get rid of the net, it might not be too bad." She stepped back and examined Jessica again. She nodded, and without another word, she left the room.

Kate and Mrs. Todd stood back and surveyed the gown as Jessica watched them with a worried expression.

"It's not that bad, is it?"

"You're going to be beautiful," Kate said, smiling. "I do think Kristin's right about the netting, though." She had to admit that Kristin seemed to have an eye for fashion. She dressed beautifully, though with much more flair than her cousin.

Mrs. Todd fingered the soft netting. "That would certainly update the look. But this is a very fine tulle. Very delicate. Do you have a veil?"

"Not yet. My mother was wearing a veil and a beautiful pearl tiara and matching necklace in her wedding pictures. I asked her one time if I could play dress-up with her necklace, and she said it was being kept safely in the bank. But when I asked my dad about it, he didn't seem to have any idea. I wonder if it's still around somewhere."

"Well, that would be lovely if you find it," Mrs. Todd said. "Either way, I could remove the tulle from the dress and make it into a veil." The seamstress walked around Jessica, pinching the excess fabric in the back. "And the dress is a little large. If you take it off and put it on inside out, I'll pin some tucks."

Kate started to undo the tiny buttons on the back. "Do you want to keep the roses?" she asked, pointing at small beaded flowers around the neckline.

"Oh yes. My mother loved roses, and so do I. They make the gown distinct."

"What if I take the straps off and use the neckline roses on the veil?" Mrs. Todd put her hand on her chin. "That would make the dress strapless, but the simpler lines will make you appear taller."

"That sounds wonderful." Jessica turned slowly around, gazing at her reflection in the mirror. She stood on tiptoe. "I'll wear heels, so you can leave the dress long. That will help. What do you think Kate?"

Kate loved the gown's simplicity. The silk was soft and lustrous, and without the straps and the netting overskirt, the gown would be very understated yet elegant. "I think it's going to be perfect."

Chapter Nine

Paul shielded his eyes from the sun. There was no breeze to carry his ball off course. Trace stood behind him, off to the left, and Gordon and Brian stood back by the carts. At the end of the manicured lawn, about two hundred thirty yards away, Paul saw a pond, but he wasn't concerned with the water trap. He doubted he could hit the ball that far.

It had been a while since he'd hit a golf ball, but when Danny Jenner called and asked him to take his place in the golf game he'd won at Jessica and Trace's shower so he could attend his son's football game, Paul had dusted off his clubs for the occasion. He'd golfed several times a year in San Antonio to have fellowship with some of his parishioners, but he was no Tiger Woods.

Trace didn't appear to be a golfer either, judging by his shorts and T-shirt and his beat-up golf bag. Gordon and Brian, on the other hand, were dressed in name-brand polo shirts, chinos, and top-of-the-line golf shoes. Their clubs looked new and expensive. Gordon even had his own custom-made golf carts with the Mackenzie Resorts logo emblazoned on the sides.

The green had to be around a corner, Paul thought, but he couldn't see a flag. He planted his feet slightly apart, a couple of feet back, flexed his knees, and brought back his three wood, ready to swing.

His arc felt right. The wood connected to the ball, and he followed through on the swing, looking up at the last moment to watch his ball sail down the middle of the fairway. About a hundred yards down, the ball sliced to the left, going into the trees. He groaned, bent down, and picked up his tee, then stepped back.

"Looks like I'll be hunting for that one."

Trace stepped forward. "I may be joining you. It's been a while."

He set up, looked down the fairway, then swung with confidence. The ball sailed high and straight, landing in the center of the fairway and bouncing toward the pond, stopping a good ten yards before the water. He whistled.

"Nice shot," Brian said, coming up behind him. "Doubt I can top that."

Brian set up, gave the course a cursory look, then took his shot. His ball landed a few yards short of Trace's.

Gordon's shot bounced left toward the trees. "I think I'm in the rough," he said, shaking his head.

The four men got in the carts and drove down to the spot where Paul's ball had disappeared into the trees. Trace helped him search for it while Gordon and Brian stayed with the carts.

There was no sign of the ball. It seemed to have disap-peared. "Perhaps I should just give up and take a stroke," Paul said.

"Hang on." Trace held out his hand, sweeping the area. Paul saw he had some kind of gadget in his hand.

After a couple of minutes, Trace called out, "Over here. I think this is yours."

The ball had bounced off a tree and landed in a dip between trees partially covered by leaves.

"Oh wow, I thought it was lost for good. Thanks." Paul took a closer look at the gadget in Trace's hand. "Is that some kind of ball locator?"

"Yeah." Trace held it up so Paul could see it.

"How does it work? I'm just using cheap balls."

"It works with digital imaging," Trace said and slipped the gadget into his pocket.

"Pretty neat." Paul recalled seeing similar gadgets for sale in a pro shop in San Antonio. He knew they were expensive. Trace was a techie, so digital gadgets would no doubt appeal to him, but for someone who hadn't golfed in a long time, it seemed odd that Trace owned one. How could he afford something like that?

Trace smiled at him, then Paul turned and surveyed his shot. If he hit the ball just right, he'd get through. Otherwise, the ball would ricochet off the trees.

"Try popping it out with a wedge," Trace advised.

Paul looked out along the path through the trees. "*Hmm.* Not what I'd pick, but why not?" He took out his wedge and lined up for a short shot. He swung. The ball popped up, barely skimming the bottom of the branches, and landed on the fairway, bouncing several times before it rolled to a stop. "Hey! Worked like a charm," he said, smiling.

Trace gave him a sheepish grin. "I had lots of experience hitting off the course back home. I played in school."

"So you used to golf a lot?" Paul asked, adjusting his first impression as they got into the golf cart and began to drive toward Gordon, whose shot was next.

"Yep, I used to, before college, on an intramural team. Nothing fancy, but I got pretty good at it."

Paul laughed. "Well, it seems like you can hold your own with your future father-in-law."

"If only I could win his approval with just a game of golf," Trace said, shaking his head. "Looks like he's made up his mind, though, and I'm a few strokes short of a hole in one." Trace looked down at the floor of the cart. "I just want him to trust me. I even told Jessica I'd sign a prenuptial agreement, but she refused." He moved his gaze out to the course. "She says to give her father time, but I don't know. I love his daughter, and I want to take care of her."

"What if you explain to him what happened with your job?" Paul snuck a look at Trace, trying to read his expression as he stopped the cart.

Trace didn't answer Paul. He just turned and jumped out of the cart, his face hidden from Paul. He waited for Paul to join him, kicking at the lush green grass.

Paul came alongside him, and they began walking toward the other men.

Trace shook his head. "Can't do that. And I doubt he'd believe me anyway."

Paul opened his mouth to ask another question, but

Gordon came up behind them and slapped his back. Paul was forced to turn his attention back to the game.

Although they were playing as a foursome, Gordon and Brian kept a bit apart from Paul and Trace for the rest of the afternoon. Gordon was footing the bill and made sure they enjoyed the golf and lunch at the clubhouse, but Paul had hoped for a chance to get to know him better. Apparently Gordon had lumped Paul together with Trace, and it was clear he didn't intend to extend a family welcome to Jessica's fiancé or her pastor. Paul knew this family needed help. He didn't know how he could facilitate bringing them together, but he knew how important family support was to a successful marriage, and he felt compelled to try. Considering the wedding was just over a month away, he didn't have much time.

THE CHOIR WAS SINGING "Blest Be the Tie That Binds" when the door to the sanctuary opened and three people came in. Kate heard Renee Lambert gasp. Kate followed Renee's gaze, watching over the top of her hymnal as Jessica, Brian, and Kristin walked three-quarters of the way down the aisle, then slipped into a half-empty pew. Brian stood in the middle. Jessica opened a hymnal and handed it to Brian so they could share it, but Jessica was the only one who joined in the singing. The other two just listened.

After the choir sang a special piece, the members filed down to sit in the front pews for the sermon. Kate ended up in the second row, two rows in front of Jessica and her companions. She could hear them whispering, but she couldn't make out what they were saying. They were quiet during

Paul's prayer, but a few minutes into the sermon, Kate heard more whispering. She was tempted to turn around and see what the fuss was about when she heard a "shush!" After that, the whispering stopped.

After the closing song, as the congregation rose and began to leave, Kate caught Jessica's eye, then saw Kristin and Brian start down the aisle toward the door. Jessica waited for Kate.

"Good morning. How are you?" Kate asked.

"I'm fine." She looked toward her companions, then back at Kate. "Sorry we were late and so noisy coming in. Kristin decided to join us at the last minute, so we had to wait for her."

"It's nice to have them here. Where's Trace?"

"He had to work." Jessica sighed. "They had some kind of technical problem, so he had to go in."

"That's too bad. Tell him we missed him."

"I will." Jessica looked around the small church. "The service was lovely. You sing so well."

"I don't know that I do, but it's fun to be part of the choir anyway," Kate said, laughing. "Jessica?"

The girl looked at Kate, her eyes wide with anticipation.

"Have you thought any more about talking to the police about your trust fund and those suspicious transfers?"

Jessica shook her head. "I'd really like to avoid it if I can. I don't want . . ." Her voice trailed off, and she looked around the sanctuary again. "I just want to keep the whole thing quiet."

"I understand, but I really think—"

"Well, I'd better catch up with Brian and Kristin," Jessica said, looking toward the back of the sanctuary, where Kristin was leaning in close to say something to Brian. "We're going out riding this afternoon. I'll see you Tuesday night."

Kate watched Jessica join her companions. Kristin had her hand on Brian's arm, but when Jessica caught up with them, he draped his arm over Jessica's shoulders in a casual way. Kristin frowned but kept ahold of his arm as they walked to Jessica's car. As they drove away, Kate thought it was a shame that Trace wasn't with his fiancée in church, but sometimes work required extra hours. At least, she hoped that was all that was going on.

KATE SLIPPED OUT OF BED at her usual early hour on Monday morning, moving quietly so she wouldn't disturb Paul. An isolated cloud hid the half-moon, barely up over the other side of the house, allowing Kate a view of the stars outside the kitchen window. As she ground fresh coffee beans and peered out into the darkness, she hummed "Morning Has Broken," anticipating the day ahead. She had an open day, and she wanted to get started on ideas for some new stained-glass projects for the Christmas season.

The rich, invigorating coffee aroma woke her senses. Kate opened the window and let the cool breeze kiss her face. She loved autumn in Eastern Tennessee, with its rich colors and crisp air. The peak of fall color in Copper Mill was nearly a month away, but the early October weather held the promise of change.

With a hot mug of coffee, Kate settled into her favorite rocking chair in the living room and opened her worn Bible to Matthew chapter six, where she'd left off reading the day before. She came to verse nineteen, and after she read it, she reread it out loud: "Do not store up for yourselves treasures on earth, where moth and rust destroy, and where thieves break in and steal."

The verse gave a warning that was directly applicable to what had happened to Jessica and her trust fund. Someone had set his or her heart on Jessica's money. Who was it, and what was the thief's motive?

There were so many possibilities Kate had considered several times over. Both Monica and Kristin had opportunity, and perhaps jealousy as a motive. From what she'd witnessed, Kate suspected Kristin wasn't as well off as her cousin, which could be another motive.

And what about Brian? He lived in New Mexico, but he and Gordon apparently did business, so it was possible that he had access to the money. Then there was Anthony, if Flora and Bertie's suspicions had any basis in fact.

And if it was Trace, as Monica had suggested, then Jessica needed to know so that she could end the engagement. If not, then Jessica's father needed to know his future son-in-law was innocent. Kate felt particularly concerned about that possibility, since she and Paul were mentors to the couple.

What about Gordon? What reason would he have for stealing from Jessica? Kate couldn't think of a single thing. The man was by no means lacking for wealth, and his deep affection for his daughter made Kate highly doubt that the man had stolen his own daughter's money.

Kate considered Henry Balderson and his secretary. The pair kept detailed records, and the firm's reputation was impeccable. Kate had seen the records they kept, and everything seemed perfectly legitimate.

Kate put her head down and read further in her Bible. The final part of the chapter was about not worrying, but she couldn't get the situation out of her mind. Trace's refusal to discuss the bank job he'd lost came back to mind, but it didn't make sense. Wouldn't he want to clear himself with Jessica and his future in-laws?

Skimming down to chapter seven, she read, *Ask and it will be given to you; seek and you will find; knock and the door will be opened to you. For everyone who asks receives; he who seeks finds; and to him who knocks, the door will be opened.* Yes, Kate decided. That's what she had to do. Keep seeking, for Jessica's sake. Keep asking. Keep knocking on doors. Someone knew what had happened during that bank fiasco. The articles she'd read mentioned an associate of Trace's. Maybe he knew what happened. Kate had to find out.

Kate closed her Bible and bowed her head. *Lord, you know how concerned I am. Please shine your light to reveal Trace's innocence or guilt and help me uncover the truth and the one who took Jessica's inheritance. Amen.*

Kate's thoughts remained on the mystery as she got dressed and then fixed breakfast. She decided to postpone her stained-glass project again and head to the library. She had to track down Art Franklin. Hopefully, he would be able to shed light on the situation.

Chapter Ten

Kate settled down in front of one of the library computers. Several people had been downstairs browsing the shelves, but it was blissfully empty on the second floor, and she turned her thoughts to her task.

Jessica had told Kate she wasn't ready to involve the police. Did she, deep down inside, suspect Trace? Had Monica's accusation planted any doubt in her mind?

Please don't let it be Trace, Kate prayed as she logged on to the Internet. Then she amended her prayer. If Trace had stolen Jessica's money, he needed to be caught, and Jessica needed to know the truth. If not, he needed to be cleared. "Please help me discover the truth. Amen," she whispered out loud.

Kate pulled the printouts from her last visit to the library out of her purse and smoothed the crumpled edges. She scanned the article for Art Franklin's name, typed it into the search window and waited.

Nothing came up. *Keep looking,* Kate reminded herself. She typed "Appomattox Commercial Bank Corporation" into the search engine and found the bank's Web site. The bank had branches all over the Southeast. Kate decided to jot down e-mail addresses and telephone numbers for all the branches in case she had no luck tracking down Art Franklin through the Lynchburg branch.

The bank site had a calendar of community events. Kate was impressed by all the charities the institution supported. A list of events included a 5K race for cancer, a blood drive, a bowl-a-thon to raise money for a local firefighter who'd been burned, the Special Olympics, and Secret Santa Christmas projects.

Kate remembered Trace mentioning the Special Olympics. He'd included donations to the organization in his budget and said he'd been supporting it for some time. She didn't know if it meant anything, but she filed that thought away for consideration.

Then Kate remembered seeing Jessica and Brian out riding horseback. How did Brian fit into all this? She searched for his name and found pages and pages of referrals to Brian Levy, owner of Arroyo Robles Thoroughbred Ranch in Ruidoso, New Mexico. Clicking on the ranch's site, Kate found pictures of beautiful, proud horses for sale or breeding. The ranch offered boarding, training, and stud service. A list of champions attested to the ranch's success, and a picture of a large indoor arena showed horses being led around a ring.

She clicked on the home page and gasped. The page listed the ranch's owners as George and Brian Levy and Gordon Mackenzie. Kate stared at Gordon's name. That little fact changed the picture.

Bertie had mentioned that Brian and his father had a

horse ranch, and Brian had been in town to discuss horses with Gordon, but she hadn't realized that Gordon actually owned a stake in Brian's business. With Gordon's hand in the pot, there was much more going on than Brian and his father simply boarding and training Gordon's horses.

Was Brian pursuing Jessica because of business interests? Marrying into the family could certainly change his whole situation. Kate pictured Brian and the way he had looked at Jessica in church on Sunday. Was his interest in Jessica genuine? Or was it strictly practical? Either way, marrying her would be to his advantage, but Jessica was now out of his reach unless he could convince her that Trace was a thief.

Kate stared at the screen for a minute, then gathered her information and went downstairs. Livvy was in her office. The door was open, so Kate stuck her head through the entry.

"Hi, Liv. How's your day going?"

"Good. Slow." She laid a pen down on her desk. "Got time for coffee? I need a break."

"Always."

Livvy rose, and Kate followed her to the employee break room. They helped themselves to the rich brew and sat at the small table with their mugs.

"How did the dress fitting go?" Livvy asked, inhaling the soft steam that rose from her mug. "Is Amelia's wedding dress going to work for Jessica?"

"It's going to be beautiful." Kate took a sip of coffee and let the hot liquid slide down her throat. "Her cousin Kristin had an odd reaction, though. I gather her tastes are more like Monica's."

"Really? She loved the frilly dresses Amelia used to buy

for her when she was little. She always dressed exactly like Jessica, as if they were twins."

"They don't seem to have the same style these days," Kate said, thinking about the red watch and Jessica's penchant for pink. And Kristin had eyed all the designer dresses with avid interest, while Jessica hadn't liked any of them.

"No, I guess not. Isn't it interesting how people change?" Livvy ran a finger around the rim of her mug. "The Mackenzies always treated Kristin like a daughter. Jessica and Kristin would enter events at the county fair together. Kristin rode fast and jumped high and always placed, but Jessica was the one chosen Fair Junior Queen, then Queen. She'd win top ribbons in every event."

"It must have been tough for Kristin to always feel like she was in competition with her cousin." Kate stared down at her coffee. "What happened to Kristin's parents?"

"Kristin's mother is a single mom. She's Gordon's sister. After Amelia died, I think he hoped that sending her to boarding school with Jessica would help Kristin adjust to her loss."

No wonder Kristin seemed jealous of Jessica. She was the poor relative nearly forced to be Jessica's companion. Gordon might not have meant it that way, but young girls were sensitive.

"Things will change after Jessica gets married," Livvy said. "Their lives will go in different directions."

"Which should be good for both of them," Kate added. She had watched Kristin vie with Jessica for Brian's attention. Just how far would she go to compete with Jessica?

"Appomattox Commercial Bank," a voice answered. "How may I direct your call?"

"Hello. I'd like to speak with Art Franklin, please," Kate said. She sat at the kitchen counter, a notepad beside her on one side and a cup of tea on the other.

"Do you know his extension?"

"No. I believe he works in the encoding department."

"I'll transfer your call. Have a good day," the voice said. The phone went to a recorded message describing all the services the bank offered. The message repeated once, then elevator music came on. Kate tapped a pen on the counter as she waited on hold.

After a few minutes, a man's voice came on. "Encoding Department. Ted speaking."

"Hi, Ted. My name is Kate Hanlon, from Copper Mill, Tennessee. I need to speak with Art Franklin, please."

"Art doesn't work here anymore."

"Oh. Do you know how I can reach him?"

"Sorry. I couldn't give out that information if I did know, but I don't. I think he moved out of town."

"Oh. Well, thanks anyway. In case you should run across him, will you take my number and pass it on?"

"Sure. Haven't seen him in two years, but I'll hang on to it."

Kate left her name, phone number, and e-mail address, just in case, then hung up.

She tried the other branches of the bank but got the same response. Art Franklin no longer worked for the bank, and no one knew where he was.

Chapter Eleven

I don't know where Trace is," Jessica said, twisting her hands in her lap. "He's not usually late."

"I'm sure he'll be here soon," Paul said. He checked his watch anyway. "Kate tells me you started working at the elementary school yesterday. How is your first week going?"

"It's great so far. Well, mostly great. I have a couple of overactive boys in the class, and getting them to sit still through a whole period is a challenge." Jessica let out a laugh. "But somehow we managed to get a little bit of schoolwork done."

Paul chuckled. Kate pictured pandemonium, but Jessica seemed happy to be working.

"But the strangest thing happened when I got home from work today. There was a little envelope on my dresser with a small key inside. But I don't know what the key is for."

"An envelope?" Kate leaned forward. "What did it look like?" Her mind flashed back to the scene in the attic. It had to be Flora's key. But why would the woman be so secretive about it then, only to give it anonymously to Jessica now?

Jessica reached into her purse and pulled out a little yellowed envelope. She handed it to Kate.

Kate recognized it immediately. The envelope was plain except for a small pencil notation in the corner: 686. Kate opened the envelope and slid the key out. It was small and old-fashioned, but surprisingly heavy. She studied it for a minute, then a smile broke out across her face. She knew exactly what the key meant.

"Sorry I'm late," Trace said, bursting into Paul's office. "There was a problem at work, and then a traffic jam, and it took longer to get here than I thought. He kissed Jessica on the cheek and settled down in the chair next to her. "So, what did I miss?"

"We might as well launch right in," Paul said, tapping a pencil on his knee. "Since we're running behind."

Kate nodded and handed the key and the envelope back to Jessica. She'd have a talk with Jessica about it later.

"We're talking about family relations this week," Paul said. "Trace, you've met Jessica's father and stepmother. Jessica, have you met Trace's family?"

"Yes. We went to Kansas over the Fourth of July holiday. They were wonderful. Everyone treated me like I was one of the family. I love how tight-knit they are." She looked over at Trace. "So different from my family, I'm afraid. I just wish they trusted us," Jessica said, shaking her head.

Trace sighed. "I'm the one they don't trust. I'll just have to prove myself to them. In time."

"They'll come around," Jessica said, reaching out to Trace.

Kate only hoped Jessica was right. But without evidence of Trace's innocence, how would Gordon learn to trust him?

DURING HER DEVOTIONS Wednesday morning, Kate's thoughts kept going to the strained relationship between Trace and Jessica's family. Through all her years as a pastor's wife, she'd mentored many women who lived with fractured relationships. In this case, as in many, the problem hinged on money. Kate knew that most conflicts involved misunderstandings or misinformation. She needed to find a way to bring out the truth, whatever it might be. *The truth will set you free*, she thought, recalling the words of Jesus.

As soon as Paul left for work, Kate headed for the library.

Please help me find Art Franklin, she prayed silently as she drove. *He might be the only one who can exonerate Trace.*

Kate arrived at the library just as Livvy unlocked the door and held it open.

"Morning," Livvy said. "You have the whole place to yourself. It could get noisy down here, though. The first-grade class at the elementary school is coming on a field trip in a few minutes."

"That'll keep you busy."

"Yes, but I love it. This is the age to catch their interest." Livvy grinned. She had such an infectious personality, the schoolchildren loved coming to the library. "I'd better go get ready."

Kate went upstairs and picked the farthest computer from the stairs. On a hunch, she began a search for Special Olympics teams in Southern Virginia. She found listings of activities and meets, and pages and pages of wonderful pictures of competitions and proud winners.

Kate had participated in a walk-a-thon for the Special Olympics in San Antonio, but she hadn't realized the scope of the organization. Athletes competed by divisions of age and ability level, and winners in each division advanced to state competitions, where the winners went on to national and eventually to international games.

She was disappointed to discover that the teams were sponsored not by individuals or businesses but by the Special Olympics organization itself. She'd hoped to find a direct link to the bank and Trace or Art Franklin. Businesses became community partners. So the Appomattox bank had sponsored employees and families who supported their fund-raiser, not a specific team.

Was that Trace's only participation during his time at the bank? To find out, she backtracked. When she searched back three years, several references came up. Kate loved the fact that the Internet data banks never seemed to expire. She located a link to an old record of the Special Olympics in Lynchburg and clicked on it.

Pictures and reports of a Special Olympics softball tournament appeared. Scrolling down through the site, she suddenly perked up. Appomattox Commercial Bank topped the list of sponsors. Excited, she started reading everything about the tournament. She found no mention of Trace Jackson or Art Franklin.

On another page, future events were listed, but they were still three years old. Kate looked through them, then linked to another track-and-field event. That didn't give her any helpful information either. Searching the pages on the event, she was pleased when pictures appeared. One of the coaches looked a lot like Trace, but the picture was grainy, and she couldn't be certain.

She read the blurb beneath the picture. Sure enough, Trace Jackson coached track-and-field events.

A group of schoolchildren came bounding up the library stairs. More sounds of excitement and energy came from the group of about twenty children. Kate grinned. Two adults appeared upstairs with Livvy. Even with the teachers or volunteers, Livvy had her hands full. As she herded the children to a conference room, she glanced over at Kate and made an expression of mock exasperation.

Kate looked at the photograph on her screen again. Trace's hand was on the shoulder of a young boy with a rounded face and small features. The names were alphabetical, so they didn't match the picture, but the name Tim Franklin appeared with the others.

Could the young athlete with Trace have been related to the man who had worked with Trace at the bank?

Kate printed out a copy of the team photo and the names. She found an e-mail address for the team and sent a note asking to be put in contact with Tim Franklin's father. She left her phone number and address as well as her e-mail address. She didn't really expect a direct response, other than, perhaps, a note stating that the organization wouldn't give out contact information. But it was worth a try. She hoped that someone would at least pass on her request.

Kate searched for Tim Franklin. She found lots of references to that name, but not regarding the Special Olympics or a young athlete. All dead ends.

She thought about how Trace and Jessica looked the previous night, so young and so much in love. She wished there was something more she could do to help them. Her mind picked over memories of the counseling session, trying to extract some detail that might clear things up.

Then it hit her. Kate almost smacked herself. In the midst of the family drama—and her confusion over Trace's seemingly apathetic behavior—she had forgotten to tell Jessica what to do with the key.

"Please pick up," Kate whispered into her cell phone. A moment later, Jessica's voice mail kicked on. She was probably still in class, Kate realized. At the sound of the beep, Kate blurted into the phone, "Jessica, take the key to the bank, ask about safety deposit boxes, and then come see me."

As Kate wandered the aisles of the Mercantile, picking up groceries and a few items to winterize the yard, she saw Sam Gorman talking to a young, tanned man near the back of the store. Sam glanced up, saw her, then gestured for her to wait a moment. He opened the back door so the young man could carry a large sack of bone meal outside. Sam walked over to Kate.

"Will you be at choir practice tonight?" he asked.

"Sure will."

"I may be late. Could you tell Renee and the others? Perhaps they can practice a cappella until I get there." The choir met at Renee's house, but Sam Gorman was their accompanist and director. "I got a special order today, and I promised I'd deliver it tonight." He nodded toward the back door, where the olive-skinned man was just walking back inside. "He's making big landscaping changes for the Mackenzie wedding," Sam added conspiratorially.

So that was the famous Anthony. "I'd be happy to tell Renee.

Practice won't be as good without your organ playing, but we'll manage until you arrive." Kate smiled. "I can't imagine how anyone could make the Mackenzies' landscaping more beautiful than it already is, though."

"They've been changing things around frequently since Anthony went to work for them, which is great for my business." Sam grinned. "He orders a lot of supplies here." They watched as Anthony hoisted another bag up on his shoulder. "I'd better go help him," Sam said, hurrying away.

Kate finished her shopping, and when she got to the checkout counter, Anthony was paying his bill. He took a wad of cash out of his pocket and peeled off several hundred-dollar bills.

Odd, Kate thought. Surely the Mackenzies had an account with Sam. Why would the gardener be paying cash? She didn't mean to be nosy, but she noticed more hundred-dollar bills in the wad as he folded it and put it back in his pocket. He looked up and saw her.

"Afternoon," he said cheerfully.

"Hi, I'm Kate Hanlon." She extended her hand. "I believe we have mutual friends, the Mackenzies."

"Friends, indeed," Anthony said. Someone whistled from outside, and Anthony turned his head. "I have to run. It's nice to meet you, Ms. Hanlon. Have a lovely day."

He left, whistling as he went down the aisle toward the back door. Kate followed him and poked her head outside. She watched him climb into a pickup truck with "D'Amico Landscaping" painted on the side. He revved the engine and drove away. He seemed to be a pleasant young man, not at all gangster-like, as Flora and Bertie intimated.

KATE CHOPPED WALNUTS at the kitchen counter Wednesday afternoon. Her mind sorted through Jessica's mystery while she waited for news from her trip to the bank.

How did Anthony fit into the Mackenzie household, and why would he pay cash for landscaping supplies? Monica and Gordon had to know he was spending money. Did he pay cash, then turn in a padded request for reimbursement? That was possible. If Gordon hadn't paid attention to Jessica's trust fund, he probably didn't scrutinize household expenditures. Did Monica watch what was spent?

Kate added the nuts and chocolate chips to the stiff batter and stirred.

Who was Anthony? He didn't look the part of a mobster to Kate, although she only had a television idea of what a mafioso looked like. Anthony seemed charming. Bertie and Flora didn't trust him, but the young man had usurped Bertie's place, so Kate couldn't give their judgment too much weight.

Kate considered Kristin again. She had an opportunity to steal Jessica's money and a long-standing rivalry with her cousin. She also loved expensive things. Kate could see her giving in to the temptation of embezzling Jessica's trust fund.

Monica seemed to think of Jessica as a rival too, rather than part of the family. That could have been motive enough to dip into Jessica's trust, couldn't it? Or was it possible that Monica stole the money to support her husband, who mistrusted Trace and opposed the wedding?

Kate was overwhelmed by the sheer number of suspects in this mystery, not to mention the list of possible motives. She also felt it was important to keep her inklings from

Jessica; the last thing the young woman needed was more confused feelings about her family.

Kate was dropping spoonfuls of dough onto a cookie sheet when the doorbell rang. She washed her hands and dried them on a towel, then went to the door. A glance at the clock surprised her. It was nearly four thirty.

Jessica stood at the door holding a pale turquoise quilted-satin box. She was dressed in a white blouse, a blue cardigan sweater, and a tweed skirt.

"How did you know?"

"Come in," Kate said, standing back. "You went to the bank?"

Jessica nodded, stepped inside, hung her coat by the door, then followed Kate into the kitchen.

"Yes. I went after school, as soon as I got your message. Mr. McKinney took me to open a safety-deposit box. Number 686. This is what was in it," she said, holding up the box.

She set the box on the kitchen table and lifted the lid. Nestled inside, on a cushion of satin, was the most beautiful tiara Kate had ever seen. Lustrous white and pink pearls and sparkling crystals set in gold surrounded an ivory cameo of a classical lady. A smaller padded box sat in the center of the box. Jessica lifted it out and opened it. A necklace of perfectly matched, pale pink pearls sat coiled inside the satin lining.

"Aren't they gorgeous?" Jessica held the necklace up against her neck. Her face glowed with joy. "I have a portrait of my mother in her wedding gown wearing these. Next time you're at the house, I'll show you. I'm going to wear them at my wedding."

"They're stunning! Your mother would be thrilled to have you wear them."

"I think so too. But you still haven't told me how you knew they were there, or how the key appeared in my room."

"You mentioned that your mother said the pearls were kept in the bank," Kate said. "When you showed me the key, I just put two and two together." Kate touched the pearls gingerly, then looked up at Jessica. "But I can't explain exactly how the key got in your room."

One thing Kate knew for sure: she needed to have a chat with Flora.

As soon as Jessica headed home, Kate pulled out the phone book, looked up the number for Bertie and Flora, and dialed. The phone rang and rang before Kate realized they were not going to pick up.

RENEE WAS PUTTING AWAY her dinner dishes when Kate arrived at her house that night for choir practice. The scent of Estée Lauder's Youth-Dew mixed with Italian food aromas filled Renee's well-decorated home.

"What are you doing here so early?" Renee said, looking at her watch as she let Kate in.

"I hope I haven't inconvenienced you," Kate said, ignoring Renee's bluntness.

"I'm not ready, but you might as well come in." Renee scooped up her pet Chihuahua, Kisses, who was dancing around Kate and pawing at her pant leg. Renee held him out to Kate.

"Hold Little Umpkins while I finish up."

Kate took the dog, who tried to lick her face. She held him firmly and scratched his ears as she followed Renee to the kitchen.

"Hello there, Kate," Renee's mother, Caroline, called from the living room.

Kate spent a few minutes chatting with the woman, then went to join Renee in the kitchen.

"Sam may be late this evening. He said to start without him and practice a cappella. He had to make a delivery to the Mackenzie place."

"Really? I wonder what he's delivering. I was there this morning, and Monica didn't mention anything. It must be for the wedding. I've been advising her, you know."

Kate nodded. Renee tended to exaggerate, but she loved to feel included.

"This was for the yard, I believe," Kate said. "Anthony was at the Mercantile when I stopped by earlier."

"Oh yes. He's intent on restaging the grounds for the wedding. He's making quite a name for himself, you know."

Kate was a bit puzzled by Renee's comment, but she didn't want to raise Renee's curiosity. "He does beautiful work."

Were the massive changes Anthony's idea and not Monica's? She'd watched him pay cash for the supplies. Why would a hired gardener be paying out of his own pocket for the landscaping? And where did he get the money?

Chapter Twelve

When Kate arrived at the Hamilton Springs Hotel for the spa day she'd won at Jessica's shower, a uniformed attendant ushered Kate to the dressing room and gave her a pale green gown, a fluffy white robe, and slippers. Soft music played in the background. Kate changed, leaving her clothes and purse in a locker. When she came out, another attendant stepped forward and led her down a hallway. Her feet sank into the plush carpet that muted all other sounds.

"Your friends are in here," she said, opening a door to an elegantly decorated lounge. "May I get you some mineral water or juice to drink?"

"Water would be wonderful. Thank you."

"Kate! I'm so glad you made it," Jessica said, jumping up from an upholstered chair. She wore a robe just like Kate's.

Monica looked displeased at Jessica's enthusiastic response, as if she'd made a social gaffe, but luckily Jessica didn't notice. Monica turned back to Renee, seated next to her, then took a sip from a china cup. Kristin was on the other side of Monica, listening to their conversation. Renee looked up and gave Kate a smug smile.

"Good morning, Kate. Nice you could join us," Renee said, greeting her as if she was the hostess.

Interesting that Renee hadn't mentioned she would be there, Kate thought. She wondered how Renee had finagled an invitation—and where she'd left Kisses.

"Hello, Kate. Looks like the party can start now," Monica said in a dry tone, making Kate feel as if she'd held them up, though in truth she was five minutes earlier than the time she'd been told.

Jessica rolled her eyes at Monica's comment, then smiled at Kate. "Come sit with me," she said, waving her over to an empty chair beside her.

Just as she sat down, five attendants came into the room.

"Good morning, ladies," one of them said. "We're so glad to be able to serve you today. I'm Jenny." She introduced the other masseuses, then went on. "You'll each receive a massage, a facial with a special pumpkin-papaya mask, then a pedicure and manicure to complete your treatment, followed by a light lunch in the Bristol's tearoom. Kate, if you'll come with me, I'll be giving you your massage today."

Kate followed Jenny to a private room. Soft lighting and music set a relaxing ambiance. The subtle scent of blackberry and sage soothed Kate's senses. As Jenny massaged her shoulders, Kate felt the kinks release. She hadn't realized her muscles were tense.

After the massage, Jenny gave Kate a glass of cold water and returned her to the lounge. Monica and Renee were waiting for their next appointments. Kate sat across from them.

"That was wonderful," Kate said. "I didn't realize my muscles were so tight."

"You need regular massages to stay in shape," Renee said. "It helps circulation and the immune system, you know."

Kate knew Renee was a regular at the spa. "I'll remember that," she said, though Kate knew the spa would remain a special-occasion treat for her.

"Monica and I were just discussing the wedding plans," Renee said in her low, raspy voice. She took a sip of imported water, then stretched her hands above her head, wiggling her shiny, French-manicured fingernails. "I find these luxurious surroundings enhance the creative processes."

Kate smiled graciously and started thinking about how she could help negotiate a truce between Jessica and her stepmother.

Lord, please intercede between Jessica and Monica so they can find common ground and a united purpose. Bring them together to become a family. If there's a way I can help, please show me. Make it clear, 'cause right now, I don't see how, but you can do all things. In Jesus' name. Amen.

Jessica and Kristin came back into the room at the same time. Kristin immediately went to the far side of the room, distancing herself from Jessica, who started telling Renee all about her mother's pearls.

Kate couldn't help wondering what was going on in Kristin's head. She and Jessica had grown up together. She was one of Jessica's bridesmaids, yet she'd aligned herself with Monica. The room was quiet, but somehow the tension was palpable. Kate was relieved when the attendants came to take them for facials.

ON MONDAY MORNING, Kate turned her studio into a photography set. White sheeting covered the worktable and frame that surrounded the wire-ornament tree she'd hung with samples of her stained-glass Christmas ornaments for the coming season. She'd already taken photos of a leaded cornucopia and Thanksgiving pieces, as well as a few items left over from her summer garden series. Her son-in-law, John, had instructed her on how to upload items to her Web site.

Kate clicked pictures from several angles, trying to catch the various facets of the objects. When she finished, she carefully wrapped a few pieces in tissue to deliver to Smith Street Gifts.

Plugging her digital camera into her laptop computer, she spent the rest of the morning uploading the pictures and formatting them with descriptions, enlargements and prices. It was nearly lunchtime when she printed out glossy pages of her work and slipped the new pages into clear sleeves in her portfolio.

After lunch, Kate took her portfolio and stained-glass pieces and drove to Pine Ridge. She spent an hour delivering items to two gift stores that had made orders online, then she got back in her car and started to pull out of her parking space when she glanced across the street and saw a red Mustang convertible. It looked familiar.

Just then, Jessica's cousin Kristin came out of a pawnshop. She was putting something into her purse. When she glanced up, Kate waved. For an instant, Kate thought she'd made eye contact, but Kristin looked down and hurried to her car. She got in, started the car, and pulled out, cutting off a car coming up the street. Kate watched, perplexed, as

Kristin drove away. Turning off her engine, Kate got out, crossed the street, and went inside the pawnshop.

"Good afternoon. Can I help you?" a man behind the counter asked.

"Hi." Kate stepped up to the counter, looking at the jewelry pieces and collectibles in the glass case. "I just saw someone I know come out of here. I know she has some lovely pieces. I'd hate to see her part with something she treasured just for a loan."

"I can't disclose her transaction," the man said. "Privacy laws. And I have to hold the item for forty-eight hours. I can tell you that she didn't take a loan, but if you want to purchase it back for her, you'll have to wait until Wednesday. I'm sorry."

Kate noticed a large book laying open off to one side of the counter. She could see a page with pictures of pearl necklaces. There was also a measuring device on the counter with calipers at one end, as if the man had been measuring something small.

"Oh well, perhaps it's something she doesn't want anymore." Kate tried to sound nonchalant. "That happens. It was jewelry, wasn't it?"

"Can't give that information, ma'am," the man said.

Kate wrote her name and number on a scrap of paper and handed it to him. "If you would call me when it's available, I might be interested in buying it."

"I suppose I can do that."

"That'd be wonderful. Thank you. I'm sure you have to mark it up to make a profit. How much should I expect to pay?"

The man thought for a moment. The doubt was back in

his expression. He rubbed his chin. "I'd guess about five hundred dollars. It's an unusual piece."

Kate thought of the jewelry from the safety-deposit box.
The tiara would be worth much more, but the pearl necklace
might be in that price range at a pawnshop. "Please don't forget to call me."

He looked at the note she'd handed him. "Kate Hanlon.
You're in Copper Mill. She's from . . . from out of town. You
sure you know her?"

"It was Kristin Holloway, wasn't it?"

He didn't reply. "I'll call you," he said.

"Thanks. Then I'll see you on Wednesday."

As she drove back to Copper Mill, Kate wondered about
the jewelry Kristin had sold. Where had she gotten it? Had
she taken it from Jessica? Kate didn't want to accuse her of
stealing, but what else could she think? She'd witnessed
Kristin helping herself to Jessica's wardrobe and jewelry box
without permission. From Jessica's reaction, Kate surmised it
happened often. Could Kristin have had access to Jessica's
trust fund as well?

Kristin jumped to the top of Kate's list of suspects. Kate
hated to think that anyone close to Jessica would take her
inheritance, but she'd still be relieved if she could prove it
was someone other than Trace. That seemed like the ultimate
betrayal.

Chapter Thirteen

Kate's curiosity drew her back to the library Tuesday morning. First thing, Kate ran a search for Anthony D'Amico and D'Amico Landscaping. Several references came up. Then she found an article about Gentian Hill Manor. It listed the landscape architect as A. T. D'Amico. She clicked on the link.

The article featured spectacular pictures of the Mackenzie estate from various angles. She scanned the article; it read like an advertisement for Anthony's creative talent. It mentioned Gentian Hill Manor throughout, even showing some before pictures, which were lovely but much more traditional and taken at a time of year when the flowers were dormant. *Tricky*, Kate thought.

Flora had tried to imitate a New Jersey accent when she talked about Anthony, if Kate wasn't mistaken. Kate went to the Internet white pages. There were dozens of listings for D'Amico, which she assumed was his last name based on the truck he drove. She found a D'Amico Laundromat. She almost laughed as the thought of Anthony laundering money in a washing machine flicked in and out of her thoughts. That was as close as she found to a mobster link. A beauty shop listed P. D'Amico as proprietor. That led nowhere. Kate gave up her search.

Since she needed to update her Web site, she took out a disk of photographs of her new stained-glass pieces that she'd brought along. Within the hour, her Web site was ready for holiday business. She then thought about trying to list some of her leftover summer items on eBay, thinking Christmas shoppers might buy them. She went to the Web site, curious.

A list of categories came up. She meant to click on "Art," but her cursor hit "Antiques" instead. She moved her cursor to go back to the previous page. As she clicked, an object on the right side of the screen caught her attention. It was gone in an instant as the screen went to the previous page. Curious, she returned to the antiques page.

The item that had caught her attention was a thumbnail picture of a figurine. It looked familiar. She clicked on the small picture. It took her to a listing of a Dresden figurine. An old-fashioned gentleman with a ruffled ascot, holding a tricorn hat, seemed to be bowing. His hair was puffed up and held in back by a ribbon. She noticed the striped pants. That was just too coincidental. She'd recently seen that same figurine, if she wasn't mistaken. The minimum bid was ninety-nine dollars.

She scrolled down to see the information on the seller. Florabunda was listed as a power seller. Kate was familiar enough with eBay to know it took lots of sales to become a power seller. She also knew that the word *floribundus* stood for a rose, but the seller's name was misspelled.

Item location: Copper Mill, Tennessee, United States.

It had to be Flora. Now the second satellite dish made sense. Flora must have needed high-speed Internet to upload files and trade items on eBay.

Had Kate just stumbled on something significant?

The seller had a store. Kate clicked onto the link. It took her to Florabunda's Attic. There in front of her eyes was the curtsying lady Dresden figurine that she'd seen in Flora's kitchen.

Kate browsed through the merchandise. The store had a selection of handcrafted window boxes, planters, and composters. She wondered if Bertie had made them. There were kits for building raised beds and instructions on planting a raised-bed kitchen herb garden, with photographs of Flora's garden.

Then Kate found several used small-garden implements. She knew people who shopped yard sales and flea markets, then resold their purchases for a profit. Perhaps Flora and Bertie did that, but she couldn't help wondering if some of their items, like the Dresden figurines, came from the Mackenzie estate. And if they were selling the estate's castoffs, did Gordon or Monica know about it?

She thought back to Flora's words. She'd said that Gordon told Flora to take all the furnishings, and he didn't care what she did with them. It seemed they had his blessing.

Kate wasn't sure the discovery gave her any useful information, but she jotted down the name of the seller and store.

Kate tapped her fingers on the computer keys as she thought about all the people surrounding Jessica. Brian Levy came into her mind. Something about him didn't sit quite right with her. How did he fit into the puzzle? She'd seen him in church again Sunday. Why was he still in town? She pulled up the site for Arroyo Robles Thoroughbred Ranch. She scrolled through the ranch's directory of stallions available for stud service. The listings gave impressive statistics. She nearly choked at the prices. The top stallion listed offspring at $80,000 for a live foal and $236,000 for a yearling. She knew thoroughbreds were expensive, but two yearlings would more than replace the trust funds Jessica had lost.

Of the horses listed, three belonged to outside owners, Brian and his father owned one, and Gordon owned the fifth stallion, Fleetfoot Mac. Interesting name. Though it reminded Kate of a popular singing group from the seventies, the Mac probably stood for Mackenzie.

Fleetfoot Mac's rankings showed that he'd won several races and placed in others. His pedigree looked impeccable. He was marked as not available for stud. Though Kate didn't know a lot about thoroughbreds, she thought offspring would increase the horse's value. Surely Gordon stood to make a great deal of money off him. Perhaps withholding the stallion from service was temporary.

All of the information on the Arroyo Robles Web site pointed to the fact that Brian Levy was successful and respected. Kate had been impressed by his manners and apparent loyalty. Gordon Mackenzie had invested in him by helping Brian and his father start the ranch. Was Gordon trying to keep that investment in the family? Was that the reason Brian was still in town? Was this Gordon's way of trying to save his daughter from marrying a man of questionable character?

Any loving father would want to protect his child from

heartbreak. Kate loved her son-in-law and daughter-in-law as if they were her own children. She and Paul had prayed for each of their children's future spouses, and God had blessed each child with a wonderful, loving partner. But what would Paul have done—what would she have done—if there'd been a question of honesty or trust? She suspected that Gordon must feel very torn, wanting his daughter's happiness while believing she was looking in the wrong place.

As Kate logged off the computer, she mentally listed what she knew. Gordon and Monica distrusted Trace. Flora and Bertie didn't trust Anthony, yet the retired housekeeper and gardener seemed to be taking advantage of the Mackenzies' generosity. Kristin took advantage of Jessica and Gordon, it seemed. What a tangled ball of strings, and poor Jessica was caught in the middle.

How could Kate help unwind the mess? Somehow she had to find the end of the string. And she couldn't stop thinking about Brian and how he fit into the puzzle. Was he somehow caught up in circumstances like Jessica? Whether he would help or hinder the outcome of those circumstances remained to be seen.

"I ASKED MY FATHER AND MONICA to come to a session with us, Pastor Paul, but they turned me down. Monica said she's too busy, and Dad said it's not necessary." Jessica sighed. "I don't think things are fine, but I don't know how to change it. Dad still believes I threw away my trust fund."

"I'm sorry to hear that," Paul said. "I would have loved to have him here. Remember, there's very little we can control in this life, but we can control our reaction to circumstances and events, and we can control our choices. The beauty of it is that those two things will positively effect the outcomes."

"Trace and I have talked about that," she said, smiling at her fiancé. He took her hand. "We're going to make decisions together, and we'll work on my dad and Monica. They'll come around eventually."

"I figure they'll come around as soon as we present them with a grandchild," Trace said with a laugh. "But we're not in a hurry. We want to get on our feet first."

They spent the rest of the session working through making decisions and handling misunderstandings. As they role-played, Kate thought of some of the situations she and Paul had faced over the years. Their in-laws had blessed them both, but there had been conflicts. Kate realized, looking back, that she and Paul had grown closer as they'd worked together to resolve those issues.

Kate was once again grateful she and Paul had had a strong and loving family support system. She prayed Jessica and Trace would have that help from his family, if not from hers.

As Kate put on her jacket at the end of the session, Jessica came over to her.

"Kate, I was wondering if you've learned anything about my missing money."

"I have some leads, but nothing conclusive yet." Kate didn't want to cast suspicion on anyone without positive proof. "But don't worry. I won't give up until the truth comes out."

"Oh, I'm not worried. Just knowing you're investigating is allowing me to focus on wedding planning." Jessica gave Kate an appreciative smile and put her thumbs in her back pockets.

"And I feel like . . . like you're trying to protect me. I have to tell you . . . it's the best wedding gift you can give me."

"Well, I have never been able to resist a good mystery, and this one's a doozy," Kate said.

Jessica was right, Kate thought. She *was* trying to protect the young woman. But mostly, she was trying to keep her from suspecting her own fiancé, unless it became absolutely necessary.

Jessica nodded slowly and was quiet for a moment. Finally, her head shot up as if she had an idea.

"Do you ride horseback?" Jessica asked.

Kate shook her head. "I haven't in years."

"Would you like to come riding with me sometime? I can remind you what to do. Maybe tomorrow afternoon after I get home from teaching?"

"I'd love to, but I've never ridden in an English saddle."

"No problem. We have Western saddles. We'll both use them."

"Oh." Kate scratched the crown of her head. "Okay. I'd like that." It would be a chance to get some exercise and, perhaps, some answers. "Oh, by the way, Jessica. Have you shown the tiara and necklace to the dressmaker yet?"

"Not yet. I have a fitting Friday after school. I thought I'd show her then. You'll come, won't you?"

"I wouldn't miss it. Out of curiosity, did you end up taking the jewelry back to the bank?"

"No. It's in the bottom of my mother's chest that I had moved from the attic to my bedroom. I put it there as soon as I got home."

Kate just nodded. She didn't want to alarm Jessica or

make any accusations until she saw the jewelry in the pawn-shop for herself. If it turned out to be one of Amelia's pieces, she'd have to alert the pawnshop and the sheriff, but not until she knew for sure.

KATE SPENT WEDNESDAY MORNING cleaning house and doing laundry. She'd just sat down for a tuna sandwich when the phone rang. The call had Kate hurrying through lunch and rushing out the door.

She pulled up in front of the pawnshop in Pine Ridge, dreading the encounter ahead. Her lunch felt like a lead weight in her stomach. Kristin had sold a pearl necklace out-right, and the pawnshop owner had authenticated its value as far above the five-hundred-dollar price tag. Kate braced her-self for what seemed to be the inevitable. Jessica would be devastated to discover that her cousin had stolen her mother's necklace. And how could Kate not suspect that she'd also stolen from Jessica's trust fund?

Kate said a quick prayer for wisdom before she walked into the shop. The man behind the counter was an older man, not the clerk she'd spoken with on Monday.

"Afternoon. Can I help you?"

"Hi. I spoke with you on the phone an hour ago about a pearl necklace. I'm Kate Hanlon."

"Yes. You're interested in the necklace we purchased. It's a fine piece of jewelry."

"I haven't seen it yet, but I'm acquainted with the seller."

"Ah. Then allow me to show you." He went to a safe and stood in front of it while he opened it. He took out a flat velvet box and brought it to the counter. "You'll notice the superior luster and grading of the pearls, and the exceptional color." He opened the box and turned it toward her.

Kate stared. She blinked. The pearls weren't pink. They were gray. She looked up at the man, who was smiling. He noticed her confusion and frowned.

"Is something wrong?"

"Yes. No. I . . . I was expecting a different necklace. I'd assumed they were going to be pink pearls."

He checked the tag against an invoice. "No. This is the necklace we purchased on Monday. We haven't had another pearl necklace for a month. Notice the matched size and color of these pearls. They measure nine millimeters, which are less popular with the younger set. The nacre is thick. These are genuine Tahitian pearls, not dyed. Natural pink pearls are freshwater pearls. These pearls are more expensive."

Kate smiled at the man, though her thoughts still reeled. This wasn't Jessica's necklace. At least not the one she had seen. "Thank you for calling me. I'm sorry. I'm interested in a pink pearl necklace."

"No problem. This necklace will sell as fast as I list it online, and someone will buy a real treasure. If I come across a pink pearl necklace, I'll give you a call."

"Thank you."

Kate got back in her car and sat for a moment, grateful she'd been spared the unpleasant task of reporting a theft. She still needed to make sure Jessica wasn't missing a gray pearl necklace, but at least this proved some of her fears unfounded. Kristin hadn't tried to pawn Jessica's mother's necklace. But that still didn't clear her of taking money from the trust fund. That mystery remained unsolved.

Chapter Fourteen

Kate looked up at the horse's back, at the saddle high above her. My, the horse was tall. A majestic animal, sleek reddish brown with beguiling chestnut brown eyes that gazed at her patiently. That was a good thing. She hadn't ridden a horse in a long time.

The stirrup was even with her abdomen, and she had to somehow hike herself up. She hoped her arthritic knee wouldn't give out on her. She reached up for the saddle horn in preparation.

"Let me give you a hand," a deep voice behind her said.

She glanced over her shoulder. Gordon Mackenzie stood behind her, his hands cupped to help her up.

"Thank you," she said. "He's certainly tall."

Gordon chuckled. "Believe it or not, we have taller. But Rusty here will give you a good smooth ride."

Kate put her left foot in Gordon's hands. As she jumped, he gave her a boost, and she swung her other leg over the saddle. Once she was seated, she slipped both feet into the stirrups. "Thank you." She gave Gordon a smile, feeling secure, then she looked down. Way down. "Oh my." She hoped she'd be able to stay put. She also hoped that she'd be able to get back down without breaking something.

Jessica came out leading her white horse. Kate could understand why the horse won so many prizes. It was magnificent. Gordon went over and gave her a hand up. She hopped up into the saddle as if it required no effort.

Jessica was dressed in jeans and a long-sleeved flannel shirt, much like Kate's outfit, and had on well-worn, brown tooled-leather cowboy boots. Kate had dug her old cowboy boots out of a box. She wasn't sure why she'd kept them, but she was glad she found them. They were in good shape, and they gave her an extra bit of confidence in the stirrups.

"Ready?" Jessica asked.

Kate shifted a bit and tightened the strap on her helmet. "Ready as I'll ever be," she said, smiling over at Jessica.

Jessica laid the reins to the right, turning her horse. Kate turned her horse and moved into line behind Jessica. They ambled slowly out of the yard.

Looking back at the valley and the town of Copper Mill, Kate appreciated the view. Down by the pool, she spied Anthony the gardener leaning on a shovel talking with someone. The other person straightened and turned. She had on a wide-brimmed hat, but Kate recognized Monica's tall, slender figure. Monica shaded her eyes, looking toward them. Kate raised her hand and waved. She didn't get a response.

The trail meandered along a gentle slope around the hillside. Asters, coneflowers, and blue gentian still bloomed along the pathway. Red ginseng berries could be seen among tall ferns on the hillside. The gentle rocking of the horse and the warmth of the afternoon sun relaxed Kate, lulling her into a peaceful state. They rounded the hill and began a descent into a small valley. The path joined with a track that came around the hill. Jessica drew up, waiting for Kate to pull alongside her.

"I've never seen this before," Kate said, stopping beside Jessica. Below them, a canopy of soft greens, yellows, and golds spread out like a mosaic puzzle. At that higher elevation, the maples, yellow buckeyes, birch, and bitternut hickory trees had become very colorful. In a couple of weeks, the scene would be even more breathtaking. "It's beautiful. A hidden valley."

"This is part of the estate, so it's not accessible by road," Jessica said. "It's called a cove forest, which means a small valley of deciduous trees. Grandma named it Gentian Cove, like the house, because of the blue gentians. She loved them. I love riding here. I brought Trace up here last weekend, and he fell in love with it too."

"I can see why." Kate let Jessica talk, hoping she might reveal the reason for inviting her along.

Jessica started forward, and they wended their way down into the trees. As the overhead boughs muted the sun, the air grew cooler. Rays of sunlight filtered down, highlighting Carolina silver bells, scarlet oaks, and eastern redbud trees.

At the bottom of the cove, a stream gurgled over smooth rocks. They crossed a wooden bridge, the horse's hooves clopping against the planks.

After a few minutes, they came to an open area with picnic tables. "Let's sit here for a while." Jessica stopped and swung down off her horse, landing with a light bounce.

Kate looked down. It was a long way to the ground. She swung her leg over the saddle and slowly eased down. Her legs hurt. It'd been too long since she'd used those muscles. She felt a twinge of pain in her knee and wondered whether she'd be able to get back up in the saddle. She hobbled to the picnic table and sat down.

Jessica took two small thermos bottles out of her saddle-bag and handed one to Kate before she sat down across from her. "Have some lemonade."

"Thanks." Kate took a drink. The cool sweet-tart drink tasted wonderful.

"This is one of my favorite places to come when I need to think," Jessica said. "It's beautiful no matter what time of year it is. I can sit here and feel like God is here with me."

Kate could still hear the water cascading over rocks in the stream. The underbrush was lush with the shiny green leaves of azaleas and a wide variety of wildflowers. She recognized lupine and columbine. "I'm sure he is. Of course, God's everywhere, but sometimes we're more attuned to him when we're alone, away from people and civilization."

"I often feel that way too." Jessica frowned. "I know we're supposed to pray all the time. My mother said all her thoughts were prayers, and she could see God in everything, even dead leaves after they turned brown. She said they were part of God's plan for regeneration as they fertilized the ground for new growth."

"Your mother was a very wise woman."

"Yeah. She told me before she died that she'd always be with me in here," Jessica said, covering her heart. "And she said Jesus was always with me. That helped. When I got

really sad and lonely, I'd picture him sitting on one side of me
with my mother on the other side. It made me feel better."

"That's lovely. Do you still do that?"

Jessica shook her head. "No. I guess I outgrew those
fantasies."

"Well, if that's fantasy, then I still indulge. I often visual-
ize the Lord next to me, comforting me or encouraging me or
showing me what to do."

"You do?"

"Yes." Kate reached over and patted Jessica's hand. "It's all
right to have your special place and your special thoughts and
memories. That's just one way God meets with us and reas-
sures us."

Kate's heart melted for this young woman who didn't have
her mother to share her thoughts and questions with.

"This must be gorgeous in the springtime," Kate said.

"It is. If it was spring now, I'd come here and pick flowers
for my wedding. As it is, Monica has other ideas. She showed
me some arrangements with these exotic miniature calla lilies
and orchids. Renee told her they're the most expensive flowers we can get, so she's all excited about it." Jessica rolled her
eyes. "I don't want to make Monica more upset than she
already is, so I'm trying to figure out if I should stand up to
her or just let it go."

"I don't know, Jessica." Kate rubbed her chin. Jessica and
Monica were headed for a showdown. Monica had Renee as
backup, and it seemed Kristin had aligned with Monica too.

"I don't want to get in between you and your stepmother,
and either way I answer, I'd be taking sides. I wonder if it'd

be more productive if we could sit down with her and discuss it? Maybe you can compromise."

"Maybe . . ." Jessica sounded skeptical.

"Why don't I invite everyone over for tea on Saturday? It'd give you and Monica a neutral environment to talk things through."

Jessica tilted her head down. "That would be great. Thanks, Kate. For everything." Jessica's eyes filled with tears. She wiped them away.

"You're welcome." Kate smiled. They sat in silence for a few more minutes, watching the sun slip lower in the sky.

"We'd better get going," Jessica said at last. "We don't want to be out in the dark. I'll lead Rusty to you. If you stand on the bench, you can get on him easily."

"Great idea." Kate smiled, relieved. "I wondered how I would get back up there."

Jessica led the horse over. "He's pretty tall, but he's such a love." She rubbed her cheek against his soft muzzle. The horse gave her a little love nip with his lips. She giggled. "I hope I can keep my horses. I just can't bear the thought of selling them. If I work full-time, I think I can afford it."

They rode around the back side of the hill, circling around the estate. Jessica pointed out other trails through the forest and a natural pond on the far side of the cove. Eventually they rounded the hill and looked down on Copper Mill. Kate loved the ride but thought she'd need a long hot bath in Epsom salts that night to soak the aches out of her body.

When they arrived back at the mansion, Jessica and a groom led the horses into the stalls to rub them down. Kate followed them inside and washed up, then waited, looking around the tack area. Across from the tack room was a sitting area with sturdy leather chairs, a couch, and a glass-topped table made from a gnarled, polished tree snag.

Kate went in and sat on the leather couch. Equestrian magazines sat on top of the table. A large glass display case covered one wall, filled with trophies Jessica had won over the past twelve years. Kate picked up a magazine about horse racing. It was dated the previous April. The cover showed a proud, beautiful horse standing in front of a fancy stable. The landscape looked arid. A headline identified the horse as Fleetfoot Mac, champion stud from Arroyo Robles Thoroughbred Ranch.

Kate flipped to the article. It highlighted the stallion, which had won a recent race. One picture showed the horse barreling down the racetrack. Another showed the horse with a foal next to him.

She was scanning the article when she heard male voices coming from behind a closed door. The voices rose. She heard two different voices but couldn't make out their words. A sharp noise sounded like someone had slammed something against the floor or a desk. Suddenly the door opened. Brian stalked out. Kate saw Gordon inside, watching him. Both men wore expressions of anger or frustration. Brian didn't look at Kate; he just kept walking out of the building. Gordon saw her, and his expression changed. He came out of the office.

"I'm sorry, Kate. I didn't know you were here. Little business disagreement. Nothing serious," he said. "May I offer you a soda?"

Kate gave him a sympathetic smile. "No, thank you. I need to get going soon. I just wanted to say good-bye to Jessica."

"Did you go up to the cove forest?"

"Yes. It's beautiful up there. I'd never heard of a cove forest before."

"They're peculiar to the Appalachian range. We're fortunate to have one on the property. Come riding anytime you'd like. Bring Paul. Monica and I often ride in the evening, and we have plenty of horses. If we're not available, our groom would be happy to guide you."

"Thank you. We just might take you up on that," Kate said. Perhaps a ride with Gordon and Monica would give Kate an opportunity to collect firsthand information about the Mackenzie family.

Her mind flashed back to the scene she had just witnessed between Gordon and Brian. What were they arguing over? Were they quarreling about business, as Gordon suggested, or about Jessica?

Chapter Fifteen

Just before noon on Friday, Sam Gorman set his coffee cup down on the table in the Country Diner. "I wouldn't worry too much, Paul. Young folks today have a lot of optimism, and that's not a bad thing. They haven't had to go through the struggles we faced, but they're smart. Just point them in the right direction so they'll know where to turn, and you'll have done a good job."

"Thanks, Sam. It's easy to tell people how important it is to be open and honest, but usually the lightbulbs don't come on until things get dark. I'd sure like to get that point across before those difficult times come."

"God'll give you the right words like he always does." Sam rose and started fishing out his wallet. "I'd love to stay, but I'd better get back to the store. Got a rush shipment coming in." He tossed two dollars on the table. "This'll cover my coffee."

Paul watched Sam leave, thinking of how good a friend and stalwart supporter Sam had become since Paul and Kate had moved to Copper Mill.

Paul debated leaving too, but he smelled meat loaf, and his stomach grumbled, so he decided to stay for lunch. LuAnne Matthews came by with the coffeepot.

"Looks like that cup's empty. Can't have that now. No charge for the refills. Ya'll know that." LuAnne held the pot over his cup and winked at him like she'd made a joke.

Paul chuckled. "Thanks. I think I'll order lunch too. That meat loaf smells great. And I'll have mashed potatoes."

"Comes with green beans and fried apples. And you want the potatoes smothered, right?"

He hesitated. "Better go easy on the gravy. Just a dab. Have to watch my cholesterol." He smiled up at the waitress. LuAnne was jolly and friendly and took good care of her customers.

She removed Sam's coffee cup, filled Paul's and then left to turn in his order. A moment later, the front door opened, and Brian Levy came in. He looked around, spotted Paul and gave a nod of recognition. Paul took the opportunity to wave for Brian to join him. The young man ambled down the aisle to the booth where Paul sat.

"Morning," Paul said, though it only lacked a couple of minutes to noon. He reached up to shake Brian's hand. "Care to join me?"

Brian shook Paul's hand, then slid into the booth across from him. "Thanks. Looks like the diner is full."

"Are you meeting someone? There's room for more," Paul said.

"No. I was in town and got hungry." He glanced around. LuAnne came over, poured him a cup of coffee and took his order.

"Are you enjoying your visit to Copper Mill?" Paul asked.

"Yes. I grew up here, you know. Not too many of my friends are still around, though. 'Course, Gordon's like family to me."

"He seems like a great guy."

"Yeah."

Brian's response didn't sound very enthusiastic. Paul knew that Kate had witnessed a disagreement between the two men, but that happened in all relationships.

Their orders came. Paul offered to pray, and Brian nodded, then bowed his head. Paul said a short blessing on the meal and their time together.

"I haven't attended church in a long time," Brian said, "except these past few weeks with Jessica. I miss it. With ranch chores and racing season, seems like I'm always busy."

Paul nodded. "It's easy to get out of the habit. You're always welcome, though, no matter how long it's been."

"Thanks." He bit into his crispy chicken. "*Mmm*. This place still serves the best fried chicken in the world. I told Loretta I'd buy her out if she'd come cook for the ranch, but she wouldn't have it."

Paul chuckled. "I'm glad. I'd miss her cooking." He ate a bite of meat loaf and mashed potatoes. "How long you planning to be in town?" he asked when he finished chewing.

"I don't know. A few more weeks. Things are slow at the ranch, and I need a break. Come the end of January when we start foaling, I won't get a chance to breathe, let alone leave."

"Well, Copper Mill is a beautiful place to visit," Paul said. "Where are you staying?"

"The Hamilton Springs." Brian shrugged.

"Pretty fancy."

"Yeah. Gordon suggested I put it on the ranch's account." Brian took another bite from his drumstick.

"So do you train horses like your father?"

"No. He runs the stables. He's one of the best horse trainers in the industry. I just manage the company. It works well."

Paul tried to form a picture of Brian's relationship with his father. He didn't get a sense that they were close. "It's always wonderful to discover our purpose in life. It sounds like you've found yours."

"Perhaps." He pushed the green beans around with his fork, then looked up at Paul. "How does a person know for sure?"

"That's a good question. The answer's not so simple, though. Opportunity. Desire. Aptitude." Paul gave Brian a half smile. "And a whole lot more. I always check with God. He has a plan for all of us, you know."

"Yeah, so I've heard. Jessica's mother used to tell me that. She was something special." He chewed thoughtfully for a moment. "Did you always know you were going to be a preacher?"

"I suppose so. I felt the Lord's call when I was still living at home. My pastor had a great influence on me and helped guide me along." Paul considered the young man across from him. Was he doubting his choices? Or regretting missed opportunities?

"You grew up around horses," Paul said. "Did you ever think of doing something else?"

"Not really. I guess I knew at an early age that I wanted to be around horses. They're so uncomplicated and comforting. I had an aptitude for numbers and organizing things, though, so I went into the business end. I guess that goes along with your answer. I might do some things differently. Different timing, anyways."

"Like what?" Paul asked, since Brian seemed to want to talk something out.

"I dunno. Just . . . things."

Paul felt like he was missing something, but he had no idea what. He just looked at Brian, waiting to hear what else he'd say.

"I've always believed loyalty and honor are about the most important virtues a man can have," Brian said at last. "So when do you pick one over the other? Which one is most important?"

"Whew." Paul let out a whistle. "You don't ask easy questions, do you? I'd advise you to pray. That's the most helpful way I know to get priorities straight."

"*Hmm.*" Brian pursed his lips and frowned as if a weight was pressing on his brow.

"Sometimes when I need wisdom or direction, I read through Proverbs in the Bible. There's a world of wisdom there. You might find your answer," Paul said and decided to add Brian to his prayer list. He could tell something was disturbing him, and Paul had a feeling it involved the Mackenzies in some way.

Brian's brow rose. "Good idea. I'll do it tonight."

After they'd finished their lunches, LuAnne came back to the booth. "Pecan pie and ice cream's really good today. I've got two pieces back there with your names on them," she said.

"Don't tempt me," Paul said, smiling. "I'm full. Brian?"

"No, thanks. But I'll take the check," he said.

"You sure?" Paul asked.

"It's my pleasure. Thanks for sharing your table with me."

"Next time, it's on me."

Brian grinned. "You've got a deal."

KATE WAS LEAVING THE HOUSE Friday afternoon when the phone rang. She opened the door to the garage, intent on ignoring it, when it rang a second time. It could be one of her children or Jessica with a change of plans about the dress fitting. Turning, she hurried back to the kitchen. Caller ID listed the number as unknown. She grabbed the receiver.

"Hello."

"Is this Kate Hanlon?"

"Yes, it is."

"You don't know me. I'm with the Special Olympics in Virginia. You sent an inquiry about Art and Tim Franklin." The man on the other end of the line paused. "I'm afraid I have bad news for you. Tim Franklin passed away five months ago."

"Oh no." Kate sucked in her breath. "I'm so sorry to hear that. I don't know them personally, but a young man in our church, Trace Jackson, used to work with Art. In fact, I think Trace was a coach with the Special Olympics."

"I remember Trace. Nice guy. He was terrific with the kids. Little Tim called him Uncle Trace. Haven't seen Trace in ages. How's he doing?"

"He's well. He's living in Pine Ridge, Tennessee, and he's getting married next month. My husband is one of the local pastors, and he's officiating at the wedding."

"That's cool. I'll tell Art next time I see him. He hasn't been to a Special Olympics event in months, but he's still around. He and Trace were thick."

"Actually, I really need to get in touch with Art. It's about Trace." Kate didn't know if he could help, but he seemed the best hope.

"I've got your phone number and e-mail address. I'll ask him to contact you."

"Thank you so much. This would mean the world to Trace. Could you try to talk to Art soon?"

"Sure. I'll try. I can't promise he'll get in touch with you, though. He's still pretty raw about Tim."

"I understand. Thank you for calling me back. Tell Art this is really important."

"Will do."

"I didn't get . . ."

He'd hung up. Kate didn't know the man's name or how to call him back.

Chapter Sixteen

Kate arrived at Gentian Hill Manor a few minutes late because of the last-minute phone call. The housekeeper let her in, and a second later, Jessica came bounding down the stairs.

"You're just in time. Mrs. Todd just got here. She's upstairs."

"How does the dress look?" Kate asked as she walked up the wide, sweeping stairway with Jessica.

"She had it in a big dress bag, so I haven't seen it yet. I can't wait to try it on, and I have the tiara and necklace, so we can see how they'll look."

When they entered the large dressing room, Mrs. Todd had taken the dress out of the bag and draped it over the couch, spreading out the voluminous satin skirt.

"Oh!" Jessica's hands flew to cover her mouth. Her eyes were bright with tears. "It's gorgeous." She went over and touched the gown as if it was an illusion that might disintegrate beneath her fingers.

It looked like a gown made for a princess, pure white amid the gold decor.

Mrs. Todd grinned as she lifted it. "Let's get this on you so we can see how it's going to fit. The seams are all basted in case we need more adjustments."

"I can hardly wait to put it on," Jessica said, going behind the screen. A few minutes later, she came out on tiptoe so she wouldn't step on the hem.

Kate blinked. Jessica looked just like the portrait she'd shown Kate of her mother.

Jessica went to the corner of the room that had tall mirrors. Holding up the billowy skirt, she pirouetted, turning her head to see the dress from all angles. Finally she stopped, facing Kate and Mrs. Todd.

"I love it. It's everything I ever dreamed of."

"Mrs. Todd, it's beautiful," Kate said. "Removing the tulle overskirt gives it just the right touch. Were you able to salvage the material for a veil?"

"Yes. There were ten yards of tulle. It'll make a beautiful veil. Do you have a headpiece for the veil, Jessica, or do you want me to attach a comb to it?" Mrs. Todd asked.

"Oh, I have it. Let me show you." Holding up her skirt, Jessica hurried behind the screen and came out with the satin box.

She opened the box, then set it down, gasping. She stared at the box, open and empty on the gold carpet. Her hand flew to her mouth. "They're ... gone." She turned wide, stunned eyes on Kate.

Kate was equally shocked. If Kristin hadn't taken the pearls, where were they?

"Are you sure that you didn't put them somewhere else?" Kate said, grasping at straws.

"No. They were in here when I put the box in the trunk."

"Where's the trunk? Maybe they fell out."

"In my room." Jessica turned toward the door.

"I'll come help you," Kate said.

"Could you look in the library? I put some schoolwork in there before I came to the dressing room. Maybe I dropped it there."

"I'll check."

Jessica held the skirt of her dress up and ran down the hall to her room.

The door was slightly ajar to the library. Kate stepped inside and heard a gasp. "Oh. Excuse me," she said. "I just need to look for ..." She heard rustling and caught sight of a figure spinning around. Kristin was standing in front of a gilded mirror, her back to it, facing Kate.

The mirror was large. From her angle, Kate could see Kristin's hands behind her holding the pink, jeweled tiara.

Kate gasped, then she quickly recovered and put on her sweetest voice. "Thank heavens, Kristin, you found the tiara," she said. She held out her hand. "Jessica was just looking for it. She's ready to try on the veil, so she needs the tiara. You have the pearl necklace too?"

Kristin glared but handed the tiara and necklace to Kate. "They fell out of the box. I was just bringing them to Jess, but I wanted to see how they looked." She waved her hand dismissively. "Definitely not my style."

"That's good," Kate said, trying to keep her voice even, "since they're meant for Jessica."

Kate found Jessica frantically looking around her room. "Here they are," she said.

Jessica whirled around and saw the jewelry in Kate's hands.

"Thank goodness! I was so scared someone had taken them," Jessica said, accepting them from Kate with trembling hands.

"Evidently they fell out of the box," Kate said, careful not to implicate Kristin, although the young woman looked more suspicious than ever.

They returned to the dressing room, and Kate helped Jessica put on the tiara, then fastened the pink pearl necklace around her neck. Jessica looked in the mirror. Her eyes glistened with emotion. Kate wasn't sure if it was from relief or from the realization that she'd almost lost the treasures.

"The tiara's perfect," Mrs. Todd said.

"I wonder if the dress was made for the tiara or the tiara for the dress," Kate said.

"I think it's both," Mrs. Todd said as she looked lovingly at the dress. "We'll have to preserve it carefully. Someday your daughter will want to wear this at her wedding, Jessica."

Jessica blushed. "I can't even imagine that. I just wish Mama was here to see this." The sparkle in Jessica's eyes faded.

The dressmaker had a pincushion on her wrist and a tape measure draped around her neck. She walked slowly around Jessica, checking each seam, marking a few small tucks with straight pins.

"Do you need the tiara to make the veil?" Jessica asked.

"No, no. You keep it safe. We'll attach it right before the wedding."

"I think I'll put the jewelry in the safe-deposit box at the bank until the wedding," Jessica said.

"That's a good idea." Kate was relieved that Kristin wouldn't have another chance to take the jewelry. "Are these your only pearls?" she asked.

"I have a necklace my father gave me when I turned sixteen. They're white. I think the pink pearls are better with the tiara, though. What do you think?"

"Definitely the pink ones," Kate said. She was relieved to learn that the black pearls at the pawnshop didn't belong to Jessica.

"Now, if you'll get out of the dress, I'll take it home and finish it," Mrs. Todd said. "We can do a final fitting next week if you like."

Jessica's face lit up. "Perfect! I can't wait. I'll have my shoes by then. Kristin and I are going shopping in Chattanooga on Sunday after church."

"Is everyone still coming over for tea tomorrow?" Kate asked Jessica.

Jessica nodded. "I told them we'd meet at your house at one. That's right, isn't it?"

"I'll see you then."

"Great! Thanks, Kate. For everything. I know it's going to be the best wedding any girl ever had."

ON HER WAY OUT, Kate saw Anthony's pickup parked in the driveway and decided to find him before she headed home. She found him pruning trees around the patio.

"Hi, Anthony," Kate said, coming up on him. "How are you?"

"Fine, Ms. Hanlon." He brushed his arm across his forehead. "Nice day."

"It is. Say, I saw a magazine spread of your landscaping. It's beautiful." She neglected to mention she'd seen it while looking for information about him on the Internet.

He looked down at his dirty gloved hand, then at her. "I'm glad you liked it. I chose the plants and design so it looks good all year."

"You chose well. I'm sure you've had encouraging feedback."

His smile gleamed white against his tanned skin and dark hair. He could have been an Italian movie star, Kate thought. "Yeah. I get job offers all the time. When I'm done here, I'll go make masterpieces out of other big estates."

"You're making a lot of changes for the wedding?"

"It will be my masterpiece," Anthony said, nodding.

Kate had no doubt Gentian Hill Manor would appear in landscape magazines, with glorious shots of the autumn outdoor wedding. "It must be very expensive to recreate the garden for a special occasion."

"Yes, but it's worth it." He reached up and lopped off the end of a branch.

Worth it for whom? For Gordon's reputation as a wealthy resort owner? But Gordon didn't seem to care about the landscaping. Monica liked to keep up appearances, but the grounds were already beautiful.

Kate wondered who was bankrolling the expansive landscaping. Could Jessica's trust-fund money have contributed? How could she find out?

Anthony had already turned his back on Kate and was

lopping off another branch. Kate turned to go, but a movement down by the stable caught her eye. Someone had just
gone inside, but she couldn't tell who the hunched-over figure was.

Kate decided to check it out and made her way down to
the stables. The horses were out in the main pasture, and the
groom was in the exercise pen with a colt, walking him
around in circles. Kate entered the stable, but she didn't see
anyone. The door to the office was slightly ajar, and she heard
murmuring from inside, then the unmistakable sound of a
file drawer slamming shut. A moment later, Bertie appeared
at the door. Flora was right behind him. They both looked like
they'd been caught in some incriminating act.

"Oh! Kate. You scared the daylights out of me," Flora said,
putting her hand over her heart.

"I'm sorry. I didn't mean to." Kate thought fast. "Actually, I
wanted to talk to you, Bertie." The gardener looked surprised,
and Kate continued. "I want to winterize the rosebushes at
Faith Briar, and I thought you might have some suggestions."
This was true. She did want to find out more about making
sure the plants survived the winter. "We nearly lost a rosebush
last year when we had that cold snap," she added.

The gardener looked flummoxed, Kate thought. Just like
a villain out of a Sherlock Holmes mystery. What were they
doing going through Gordon's files?

Bertie stepped out of the office. Flora followed and shut
the door behind her.

"Have you fertilized them since August?" he asked.

"I don't think so. Should we?"

"No. But keep watering them. And leave on any blooms.

That'll let them form rose hips. That's good for them, so they'll go dormant, you know."

"I *didn't* know." Kate laughed, trying to release some of the tension she felt from catching the pair in Gordon's office. "We usually take all the blooms off. It's a good thing they've survived at all."

"Then wait for a couple of freezes before you mulch them. That's about it."

"Thanks for the advice." Kate nodded. "It doesn't sound too difficult."

Flora took hold of Kate's arm. "If that's all, why don't I walk you to your car?"

"Of course." Kate had the sneaking suspicion that Flora and Bertie were railroading her to get her away from the stable, but this was working out better than she could have hoped. Kate still hadn't been able to talk to Flora about the mysterious envelope and the safe-deposit key, and Flora wouldn't be able to evade her this time.

"I've actually been trying to get ahold of you," Kate said as Flora escorted her back toward the front of the house.

Flora stopped suddenly in her tracks and turned to face Kate. "I just didn't want her to be disappointed."

Kate stepped back, trying to make sense of Flora's words.

"I know what you're thinking," Flora said, her feet crunching on the gravel driveway. "But when the key fell out of the trunk that day, I was as surprised as you were." Flora looked at Kate, her eyes wide. "I hadn't seen Mrs. Amelia's pearls in decades, but I realized that this might be the key to the lock box at the bank. I didn't want to get Jessica's hopes up, though, in case . . ." She reached out and touched Kate's arm.

"I just didn't want her to be disappointed. So I took the key and brought it to the bank. They wouldn't let me see what was inside the box, but I was fine with that. I just needed to know that the key was indeed what I thought it was."

"So why did you leave the key in her room anonymously?" Kate wanted to believe Flora, but something in the retired housekeeper's story didn't add up. "Why wouldn't you want to tell her about it yourself? Make sure she figured out what it was for?"

Flora looked sheepish. "I didn't want to tell her I'd taken the key without asking. I was embarrassed about that." She shook her head. "I should have just told her the truth from the beginning, but . . ." Flora's voice faltered. She took a deep breath. "I love that girl like she's my own daughter," she said, her eyes glistening. "The poor girl has had enough disappointment recently. I didn't want to add any more misery to her life."

Kate nodded because she didn't know what else to do, and she couldn't help but see Flora's point.

As Kate drove home, she wondered about Bertie and Flora. She wanted to believe Flora's story about the key, but what were she and Bertie looking for in Gordon's office? Why would they act as if they'd been caught doing something wrong? Could they have had access to Jessica's trust fund and stolen the money? If they cared as much about Jessica as Flora professed, they wouldn't want to hurt her. Then again, they'd be certain Gordon would take care of his beloved, only daughter.

Chapter Seventeen

Kate straightened the pillows on the couch and cast a final look around the living room. The vacuum, dust rag, and furniture polish were put away. The air smelled of fresh ground coffee, vanilla, and cinnamon.

The doorbell rang. Kate smoothed the hem of her beaded V-neck sweater over her gray tweed slacks, then opened the door.

Jessica, Monica, Renee, and Kristin stood at the door.

"Come in," Kate said. "Would you like me to hang up your jackets?"

"Oh, good, a fire," Renee said, slipping off her faux leopard jacket. She set Kisses' carrier on the floor and let out the little dog. "It's gotten nippy out."

Monica handed Kate her wool jacket. Monica looked around before she took a seat at one end of the couch closest to Renee, who had just sat down near the fireplace. Kisses jumped into her lap. Kate couldn't read Monica's expression.

Kristin sat next to Monica, leaving Jessica and Kate across from them on the love seat, as if they were divided into two opposing sides, and the odds were three to two. Kate noticed Jessica's frown and gave her an encouraging smile.

"Can I get you some coffee or tea?" Kate asked.

Jessica jumped up. "I'll help you."

Jessica took orders, then brought out drinks and small plates. Kate carried in a tray of fresh apple-nut bread slices, which she offered around, then set on the coffee table. She sat and took out her notepad.

Monica took a bite of bread. "This is good," she said.

"Thank you. I'm glad you like it. And I'm glad y'all could make it this afternoon." They chatted for a few minutes, and then Kate steered the conversation around to the wedding.

"You must have so many arrangements to finalize for the wedding," Kate said, nodding sympathetically at Monica. "How are you holding up?"

Kristin sat silently nibbling on a piece of the bread.

"It's definitely time consuming," Monica said, taking a sip of her tea. "But things are going well. I've received over two hundred RSVPs and only seven regrets." She wiped her fingertips on a cloth napkin. "I've ordered special flowers shipped in from Hawaii. They're going to be just gorgeous. We have a florist from Chattanooga who will bring them up and arrange them Saturday before the wedding. She'll have the arch, a pair of tall baskets, kneeling bench, candelabras, and a scarlet run—"

"Monica, what happened to my pink roses?" Jessica interrupted.

Monica glanced up. "I think you're really going to love these arrangements," she said, pasting a smile on her face. "I ordered a combination of coral, mango, yellow, and green exotic tropical flowers. Trust me. They'll be stunning."

Jessica pursed her lips.

Monica described all the decorations and place settings she'd ordered. "And the Bristol is going to cater dinner." Her eyes lit up as she described the meal. "There will be a five-course dinner with prime rib, smoked pheasant, and plank-grilled salmon for the entrées."

"I still don't think we need anything that elaborate," Jessica said quietly. "Honestly, a cold supper would be fine."

"We don't entertain that way," Monica said, raising her eyebrows.

"That might be fine for an afternoon luncheon, but not a formal wedding," Renee added, shaking her head.

"I just think this is all way too fancy." Jessica twisted her napkin in her lap. "All we want is to have our families and friends there to celebrate with us."

Monica waved a hand dismissively. "This is your big chance, Jessica. Your father will only pay for one wedding."

"I'm only going to have one wedding. I'm marrying for life. With God's help, we'll make it work." Jessica sighed. "I wish . . ."

Whatever she wished, she left unsaid.

"The Bristol has these gorgeous heart-shaped cakes," Monica continued, digging out a picture and passing it to Jessica.

"That's beautiful," Jessica said, studying the glossy picture. She passed it to Kate. The cake had an intricate sugar lattice and exotic flowers and bells.

Kate felt a surge of hope. Maybe the two women would agree on this, if nothing else.

"If they could leave off most of the decorations and just

use a few roses and maybe some piping, it'd be perfect," Jessica continued.

Kate thought that was a reasonable request. She passed the picture back to Monica.

"That'd insult the chef. He is famous for his intricate designs." Monica shook her head. "I suppose we could change the flowers to roses, but I won't ask him to ruin his masterpiece."

"Monica's got all these fabulous things lined up." Kristin said, looking at Jessica. "You should listen to her." She turned to Monica. "You're so good at organizing all this. I'd love to have you plan my wedding."

"Oh, are you getting married soon?" Kate asked. She remembered the way Kristin smiled at Brian.

"Not right away, but you never know," she said, giving Kate a haughty look.

Kate wondered if Kristin had some scheme up her sleeve. No doubt her plans included Brian, but in that case, she needed to get Jessica out of the way, which would happen when she married Trace. Then what? Had she used Jessica's trust fund to bankroll her plans?

Monica went on to describe more details, including music, and it became more and more clear that Monica and Jessica had distinct ideas about what they wanted. Kate wondered how it would all come together. She was glad Renee kept most of her thoughts to herself. Kristin hadn't offered any constructive ideas either, but she made a show of supporting Monica's plans. This wasn't exactly the friendly break-the-tension tea Kate had hoped for.

By the time they left, Kate felt as if she'd been through a wringer. Jessica was giving in to Monica on most accounts, but the strain between the two women remained. Kate felt sorry for Jessica. Wedding details were unimportant compared to Jessica and Trace's relationship, but time was growing very short. Kate believed Jessica and Monica could unite enough to pull off the wedding, but could they unite enough to become a family?

"I HAVEN'T HAD such strong reservations about an engaged couple in a while, Katie." Paul stood at the kitchen counter tearing pieces of romaine lettuce into a wooden salad bowl as he spoke. "I had lunch with Brian Levy yesterday. I got the impression he's concerned about Jessica. I suspect that's why he's still here."

Kate flipped the pork chops that were cooking on the stove and pressed on them with the spatula. She added sliced onions and mushrooms to the pan. "How did you happen to have lunch with him?"

"He came into the diner alone, and I offered him a seat. Seems like a nice guy. I think you're right that he's in love with Jessica."

"He doesn't really try to hide his feelings, does he?"

Paul sighed. "I wish I felt certain Jessica and Trace should marry. I just have this uneasy feeling. And it's not helping me put together my sermonette for the wedding."

Paul pulled a vegetable peeler out of a drawer and started on the carrots. "They asked for something nontraditional that will bless their marriage and invite the guests to be part of their new lives together. Shouldn't be so hard, should it? But I just don't know what to say."

"How frustrating. I'm sorry." Kate put her spatula down and wrapped her arms around Paul's neck. He hugged her around the waist and held her tight. Paul took his mentoring duties so seriously. He genuinely cared and wanted to help couples deepen their relationships. If Trace and Jessica didn't grasp the concepts and apply them, they would struggle with each other as well as her family.

Kate gave Paul a kiss, then went back to turn the meat again. "I understand how you feel. I have reservations too," she said. "I keep praying about it. There's so much distrust between everyone connected to the Mackenzies. Even if Jessica and Trace are perfectly suited, they're facing family strife."

She watched as melted butter popped and sizzled in the pan. "I was hoping to find out about that job Trace lost and try to clear his name, but I've only run into dead ends so far. Meanwhile, the list of people who could have stolen the money from Jessica's trust fund gets longer and longer every day."

"So, Trace is still on the list?" Paul was back to peeling the carrots.

"Yes."

"What about Brian?"

"I don't know." Kate stepped away from the stove and leaned back against the counter. "He seems to be wealthy in his own right. I see no motive unless he moved her money to protect her from Trace."

"Plus, I can tell that Gordon really favors Brian. Still, I'm sure he'd come around if he could believe Trace is trustworthy."

"Jessica and Trace say they've prayed about getting married, so they haven't made their decision lightly," Kate reminded Paul.

"That's true." Paul gave Kate a half grin. "So perhaps we should back off and exercise a little faith."

"Wise words, Preacher. You always say God answers prayer. Maybe we should trust him on that."

Paul held up a carrot and pointed it at Kate. "You've got a point." He took a bite off the end of a carrot.

"Not anymore."

Paul waved the pointless carrot at her and grinned.

"I TOLD JESSICA..." Trace looked over at his fiancée and smiled, squeezing her hand. "Maybe we should go along with Monica's plans to keep the peace. After all, a wedding is just one day out of the rest of our lives. If she wants to do the fancy rehearsal dinner, let her go for it. I'm supposed to pay that bill. Fine. I'll pay it."

"But she'll spend a fortune of your money—our money," Jessica said. "We can't afford that."

Jessica looked down at their hands clasped together. They were sitting in Paul's office at the church for the sixth premarital counseling session. "This is getting so complicated. Maybe we should elope." Jessica looked up, her eyes wide. "Maybe you could marry us in a private ceremony, Pastor. Then we could just do a reception and forget all this other stuff."

"It's a nice idea, isn't it?" Trace said. "But I know you better than that. You'd always regret it if the people you love weren't there." He ran his fingers lightly up and down

Jessica's arm. "You found your mother's wedding dress, and I want to see you walk down the aisle in it with our family and friends there to celebrate with us. Other than that, I don't care what happens. Let Monica do what she wants."

"But she's getting such expensive, exotic flowers, and I don't even like them," Jessica complained.

Trace pressed his lips together. For a moment, he didn't answer. Then he gave a little nod, as if he'd made up his mind about something. "Why don't you order the flowers you want. She can put hers on the tables for dinner, and we'll use what you want in the ceremony. I've got some extra savings set aside. We could use that."

"You do?" Jessica said, staring at him.

"Rainy-day fund," he said, smiling at her. "We'll manage. You should enjoy planning our wedding, not stress over it."

Jessica beamed, but Kate felt a sense of dread. So even after their talks about money, Trace hadn't told Jessica about his savings. Kate didn't understand why Trace would keep that from his fiancée, especially when financial suspicion was hanging over him. She glanced at Paul and read hesitation in his eyes as well.

Paul shifted his gaze back to the couple, and they went over the previous week's assignment, which was about personality differences. Jessica's personality test revealed that she had an otter-like temperament, which meant that she was energetic and outgoing, and Trace was like a Golden Retriever, which meant that he was laid back.

The pair admitted that some of their weaknesses overlapped, but Kate could see their resolve to make their relationship work, regardless. As much concern as she felt for them, she couldn't help but give a mental thumbs-up to the couple. Their love for each other was evident.

As Paul went over their test results, Kate thought about the little boy Trace had coached in the Special Olympics. She needed to tell him about the boy, but that meant she'd have to admit that she'd been investigating him. She'd told Jessica she would look for the trust-fund thief, but she suspected Jessica didn't mean for her to investigate Trace. Kate didn't know what to do, so she silently prayed for guidance and waited to see if she'd get an opening in the conversation.

She didn't. She decided to wait.

But she couldn't help wondering about Trace and his secret savings account. Why hadn't he mentioned it before? And where had the money come from? Was it something he got from the bank where he'd worked? Or from Jessica's trust fund?

Chapter Eighteen

It was a perfect fall evening, brisk enough for a jacket. Paul and Kate had walked home from their meeting with Jessica and Trace. As they strolled home hand in hand, the street light at the corner and the lights at the high school illuminated their way. When they turned up Smoky Mountain Road, it took a few moments to adjust to the darkness, but then the moon and profusion of starlight opened the sky before them.

"I love this time of year, when the air gets crisp and the trees turn colors," Paul said. "We should walk home more often."

Kate walked in silence for a few minutes, listening to the rhythmic crunch of gravel beneath their feet. There was something comforting about hearing Paul's steps beside hers. They'd walked a lot of miles together in nearly thirty years of marriage. Sometimes the road was smooth and level, and sometimes twisted and hilly, but always, they'd had each other. What would life be like for Trace and Jessica?

"Jessica was surprised when Trace mentioned his savings account," she said. "Evidently he never got around to telling her. I was hoping he would."

Paul looked down at her. "I'm glad he finally told her about it. I wasn't sure he would, since he wants the house to be a surprise."

"It certainly will be a surprise." Kate thought about the enormous cost of buying a house. "I wish he'd be more open about it. If I wonder where he got the down payment, so will everyone else. The Mackenzies are sure to point out the missing funds from the job he lost and from Jessica's trust fund. They already suspect him. I imagine even Jessica will wonder, though she'll defend him."

"Good point. I hope he's considered that." Paul pushed up his sweater sleeves. "I've wrestled with how much to interfere. Maybe I'll talk to him again."

"I think that's a good idea. And I've got some checking to do on Jessica's cousin Kristin. I'm hoping she'll lead me to the missing money."

KATE ARRIVED AT GENTIAN HILL MANOR at the same time as Mrs. Todd on Wednesday afternoon. Jessica had been watching for them and opened the door before they could knock. She was so excited, she could hardly stand still. Kate carried the dress bag up to the dressing room while Mrs. Todd carried her sewing kit.

Jessica pulled her hair up on top of her head and secured it in place with a clip.

"I'll have my hair done up right for the wedding," she said. She slipped on three-inch white-satin heels, then reached for the jewelry box.

"I picked this up at the bank so I can see it all together. I'll need some help with this dress," she said.

Mrs. Todd helped her slip on the dress, then fastened the pearl necklace around her throat. The seamstress stepped back and watched Jessica walk slowly around the screen and across the room to stand in front of the full-length mirrors. She moved with a natural grace.

Mrs. Todd attached the tiara to the veil and together, she and Kate fitted it on top of Jessica's head.

Just then the door opened. "I heard you're fitting your dress. Let me see..." Monica stepped into the room, then stopped dead in her tracks and stared.

Jessica slowly turned toward her stepmother. Her eyes sparkled. She looked radiant.

Kate heard a soft gasp and turned to see Monica's stunned reaction. For an instant, Kate saw a deep longing in Monica's eyes. Perhaps Monica did care for her stepdaughter, more than she knew how to express. Then their eyes met, and Monica blinked. The look was gone.

"Lovely," Monica said. "I believe it will do nicely."

"Thank you, Monica. I'm glad you like it."

"Yes, well..." Monica turned back toward the door. "I have an appointment. I...I just wanted to make sure your dress would be ready in time."

Kate glanced back at Jessica. The young woman shrugged, but her smile remained. She had seen the look in Monica's eyes too. It seemed nothing could dim her excitement at that moment. And that was just as it should be, Kate thought.

WHEN KATE WANTED TO SOLVE a problem, she baked. Something about the chopping, measuring, and mixing freed her mind to unravel complicated equations, and the puzzle of Jessica's trust fund was a doozy.

Apples had been on sale the previous Friday at the Mercantile. Kate had purchased several pounds, and what remained needed to be used up, so Thursday morning, with her mind filled with questions, she got out the ingredients for an apple-nut bread.

Jessica had told her that she drew from her trust fund using a debit card or by making electronic withdrawals or transfers. Kate also knew that the bogus transfers had been made electronically. That meant whoever made the transfers had learned Jessica's password and ID and whatever safeguards were on the account. Like most people, Jessica had used names of things familiar to her as passwords, like her horse's name, her date of birth, and her nickname. Hardly foolproof. Anyone who knew her could figure out her mother's maiden name, her favorite pet, where she was born, or where she went to school.

Kate considered, for the umpteenth time, who had the motive and opportunity as she diced an apple into a large glass measuring cup. In this case, who didn't have both? She mentally listed the names of those close to Jessica.

Kristin came to mind first. She hadn't sold Jessica's pearls to the pawnshop as far as Kate knew, but her motive and opportunity remained the same. She seemed all too interested in sharing Jessica's things, as demonstrated, among other things, by her recent game of dress-up with Jessica's pearls and tiara.

Then she thought about Gordon again, even though she had all but dismissed him as a suspect before. At this point, she needed to consider every possible angle. Gordon had access, of course, but she couldn't imagine a possible motive. He'd spent all of Jessica's life making sure she was well provided for and had all the opportunities to succeed, and he blamed himself for not keeping track of her fund and advising her or doing something to prevent the theft, which was probably why he was being so hard on Trace.

Kate picked up another apple and sliced into it.

Trace. Next to Kristin, he seemed the most likely suspect. But why would he take Jessica's money when he would gain it legally after they married? Did he have a secret debt to repay? Like the money from the bank? But he had substantial savings—at least he said he did.

What about Bertie and Flora? They adored Jessica. Why would the two former employees take Jessica's money? Maybe they wanted the money for retirement? Kate hadn't seriously considered that before. But it made sense. After all, they felt no qualms about selling the Mackenzies' castoffs. Were they stockpiling money away for the future? Although, Kate reasoned, recycling discarded goods wasn't a crime.

What about the safe-deposit box? Flora had hidden the key from Jessica, but her explanation for doing so seemed sincere.

Then there was Monica. Until the previous day, Kate had considered her a suspect. But the longing Kate had seen in Monica's eyes hinted at the stepmother's desire to break through the gulf between her and Jessica. Still, Kate wasn't convinced that Monica hadn't funneled Jessica's inheritance into Gentian Hill Manor's elaborate grounds.

Kate measured flour, sugar, oats, and spices into two large bowls. After going through her list of suspects, she decided she needed to talk to Monica first. Perhaps she could learn more about her and about Jessica's cousin. Monica had liked her apple-nut bread on Saturday, so Kate thought she'd bring her a loaf and try to make some headway with the woman.

Kate changed clothes while the bread baked. As she took two loaves out of the oven, the warm smell of apples filled the air. She wrapped one loaf in parchment paper and then a towel to keep it warm, then she headed out the door, hoping Monica would be at home.

MONICA AND RENEE were sitting in the breakfast room going through swatches of fabric when the housekeeper showed Kate into the room. Renee's dog tote sat on her lap, and Kisses' head was showing through the mesh window. Kate could hear the sound of Kisses snoring.

"Hello, Kate. This is a surprise," Monica said. "Would you like a cup of coffee?"

"Sure, thanks." Kate walked over to the two ladies and held out the tea loaf to Monica. "For you. I was baking today and remembered you liked my apple-nut bread."

"Even though you couldn't make a good cup of tea if your life depended on it, you do know how to bake," Renee said.

Kate couldn't help but smile at Renee's backhanded compliment.

"Well, thank you," Monica said, accepting the bread. "Gordon will enjoy it too." She set it aside. "Would you like to have a seat?" She gestured to the empty chair across from her and Renee, but her voice was flat. Kate got the sense that Monica's invitation was based on social propriety and not a desire for Kate's company.

"We're picking out colors and fabrics for our resort in Telluride, Colorado," Monica explained. "We're remodeling some of the condos."

"How fun. You have such a flair for decorating."

Monica looked startled by the compliment. "I enjoy decorating. It's such a challenge."

"Telluride is a ski resort, isn't it?" Kate leaned in to get a closer look at the swatches. "Do you have a theme for the remodel?" she asked.

"Four seasons," Monica said. "Skiing, biking, hunting, and . . ."

"Mud," Renee supplied.

"No." Monica gave her a playful scolding tap on the arm. "Spa season. I really want to push the off-season. We run a spa year-round, but April and May aren't the best time for activities outdoors because the ski slopes close, and it rains a lot."

"Hence the mud," Renee said. "But I'd go for the spa treatments."

"That's what we're aiming for. The town puts on artsy films and shows, and we offer luxurious relaxation."

"That sounds nice. Will you do theme rooms or try to incorporate the idea of activity seasons throughout the resort?" Kate asked, fascinated at the thought of remodeling an entire resort. She enjoyed decorating her home, but something on such a large scale seemed both exciting and daunting.

"Why, Kate, that's a grand idea," Renee said. "Pick a color scheme that's neutral enough to highlight all the different seasons, then go with seasonal artwork, like old skis or snowshoes, or spa candles. Each season, appropriate brochures and some complimentary tickets or discounts could be placed in each unit."

"Personally, I like bright colors, but I was looking at the soft teal and muted mauve for the resort," Monica said, looking at Renee. "What do you think?"

"I like it. Kate, you have decent taste. What do you think?"

Kate glanced at Monica. She saw a hint of resistance in the slight narrowing of her eyes.

"You've done such a wonderful job here, I'd trust your instincts," Kate said. "Besides, you're familiar with the resort and the goal you're trying to achieve." Kate smiled at her hostess, hoping to convey encouragement and approval. "Do you do all the decorating at your resorts?"

"Oh no." Monica shook her head. "But I like to be involved in the decisions."

"She's too modest," Renee said. "She comes up with fabulous ideas. The decorators usually incorporate all her suggestions."

"I took design in college," Monica said with a shrug. "And I travel all over with Gordon. I do most of the planning and decor for his out-of-town events, as well as the events he holds in town."

"I've been to a few," Renee said, "and they are showstoppers."

Kate and Paul had wealthy friends in San Antonio and had been to their vacation homes, but even their lifestyles were nothing like the way Monica and Gordon lived. Kate couldn't imagine traveling around as much as they did. Living in so many places would mean never feeling really settled. They were only at this house a few months out of the year, while Kate's home was her refuge.

"Do you ever get tired of the travel?"

Monica raised an eyebrow. "My folks still live in the house they had when I was born. I couldn't wait to get out and see the world. Traveling does get old though. Gentian Hill Manor is home. Gordon loves it here. Sometimes I think I'd like to stay here for an entire year."

"You should suggest it, dear," Renee said. "Gordon could use a year without the stress of the resorts."

Monica shot Renee a warning frown, as if she'd revealed too much to a stranger. "It's up to him," she said. "Meanwhile, I need to pick the decor so we can order it in time to get the work done in the off-season." She turned back to her fabric.

Kate pushed her chair back. "I'd better leave you to your work." She had gained a little insight into Monica's life, but she sensed that a wall of defense had gone up. "And I guess I should get back to mine."

"What do you do?" Monica asked. She seemed surprised to find out that Kate worked at all.

"I'm creating some stained-glass pieces for the holiday season. Stained-glass work is my hobby."

"Oh. How nice." Monica smiled but didn't look up from her fabric.

Kate left the two women in the breakfast room, went out the front door, and walked toward her car. As she opened her door, a pickup truck came around from the direction of the stables and office. It was Bertie, with Flora in the passenger seat. She was sitting with her back against the window, talking to Bertie, who was looking straight ahead. They didn't see Kate. She waited until they were down the driveway into the trees before she followed them.

Had she and Bertie been going through files in the office again? How did they get in? And just what were they looking for? Were they looking for paperwork on some of their eBay items? Or trying to discover what had happened to the missing money from Jessica's trust fund? Or something else entirely? They suspected Anthony of stealing Jessica's money. Were they looking for incriminating evidence?

Chapter Nineteen

Paul got out of his pickup and looked around the modern warehouse district in Pine Ridge. He spotted a plain building on the corner with a sign identifying it simply as the Café. Rows of blue metal buildings ran together. Each structure had a single window and an institutional steel door with large, clear numbers and a small sign giving the company name. Paul looked for the address of Trace's employer: Suite 426. Commercial Security Products.

He crossed the street and entered the building. A small reception area held a few institutional chairs and a counter.

"May I help you?" a woman behind the counter asked.

"I'm looking for Trace Jackson. I believe he works here."

"Yes. In our IT department." The woman took Paul's name and disappeared through a doorway.

Paul sat down to wait. He picked up a thick bound catalog and skimmed through it. It was filled with locking devices and parts, alarm systems, and electronics. A door opened and Trace came out.

"Hey, Pastor, good to see you. What brings you here?"

"Trace." Paul stood and shook Trace's hand. "I was hoping to catch you in time for lunch. I see there's a café down the street. Do you have time?"

"Sure do."

Trace told the woman behind the counter that he was going out, then he opened the door for Paul. They walked down the block to the café, commenting on the beautiful weather.

Once they were seated and had ordered, Paul jumped in.

"I haven't been in this part of town before. Seems like a bustling area. Lots of small businesses."

"Yeah. Pine Ridge was smart to run fiber-optic lines in here. Great communication, but the rents are much cheaper than in Chattanooga."

"You've been on the job what . . . a couple of months now?"

Trace nodded. "Almost seven weeks."

"How's it going? Do you enjoy the work?"

"Yeah. It's great . . . mostly." Trace looked around. The restaurant was bustling with customers, but no one was watching or listening to them. He leaned forward. "My project is a challenge, and I like that. Only downside is everyone comes to me to fix every other computer problem. Half the time it's really easy to fix, and I love working with computers, but it often takes time away from my real job. Even the boss does it, so I can't complain, but I end up putting in a lot of overtime."

"In seven weeks you've become indispensable. That's a good problem."

Trace laughed. "I guess it is. I need the job security, especially once I sign that mortgage. 'Course I can't tell Jessica that when she complains I'm working too much."

That was the opening Paul was hoping for. "I noticed Tuesday night that Jessica seemed surprised when you mentioned your savings. Have you talked about it?"

"I told her a long time ago that I had some money set aside as a nest egg. We never discussed how much. With her large trust fund, my savings seemed insignificant. Now, of course, that situation has changed, but I don't know, I guess it just didn't seem important to mention the amount. And anyway, I'm glad I didn't mention it, because if I did, she'd know we can afford to put a down payment on the house, and I still want that to be a surprise."

"So far, you're pulling it off," Paul said, trying to keep his tone somewhat lighthearted. "I've been impressed with your budget. You're very thorough. Not all young couples list tithing and charitable giving as part of their budgets. I was glad to see that. I can see you've been careful with your resources for a long time. Your savings must be healthy to put a down payment on a house."

"It is." Trace leaned forward over the table, and gave Paul a conspiratorial smile. "I have almost a hundred grand in a money-market account. I have stocks too, but I don't want to touch them. They're for retirement."

Paul whistled. "You're how old?"

"Twenty-eight."

"Wow. Most young people don't have nearly that much foresight."

He grinned. "I'm frugal."

"You're a lot more than frugal. Didn't you get your master's degree recently?"

"Yes, and I don't owe a dime for my education," he said, looking a little smug. "That's why I could qualify for a mortgage."

"That's quite a feat. How did you accomplish so much?"

Trace sighed. "I'm a good guy, Pastor. I wish I could get Gordon to trust me before we get married. It would mean so much to Jessica to have his blessing."

"Maybe it's time you sit down and discuss these things with Gordon. I know it's old-fashioned and not always practical, and I know you're worried that Gordon would dismiss the effort, but in this case, it makes sense. It might help Gordon respect you more, especially if you give him the opportunity to ask you questions."

Trace shook his head sadly. "He'd want to know about that bank mess, and I can't talk about it. He'd only get more set against me."

Paul frowned, trying to make sense of Trace's reticence. "I suppose that's true, unless you open up to him. How about another approach? Gordon's a businessman. Can you give him something positive—tell him about your finances and how you got there?"

Trace still looked doubtful. "Sure, if it'd do any good. I've been repairing, restoring, and building computers and electronic components since I started high school. People sell or give me their old computers and printers, and I upgrade them, then sell them. I paid my way through college that way. And I've been investing. I can give him copies of all my bank and investment statements."

Paul nodded. "Well, whatever you *can* talk about with Gordon, it might remove some obstacles. I know it's hard to set aside your pride and explain yourself, but it seems the rewards could be worth the effort."

"Yeah." Trace rubbed his neck, then took a deep breath. "Okay. I'll talk to him. About my finances."

"I'd be happy to go with you if it'd make it easier for you," Paul offered.

"Thanks, but I think I need to do this by myself." Trace straightened his shoulders and lifted his chin. "There is something you can do, though."

"Sure. How can I help?"

"Would you pray for me? You and Kate? It'd mean a lot to know God is with me when I sit down with Gordon."

"You have our prayers without asking. We've been praying for you and Jessica since the first day we met."

"Thanks, Pastor. I know it'll help."

Paul hoped his advice and prayers would help. Jessica's father might accept Trace or he might not. At least Trace was willing to reach out with an olive branch.

WHEN KATE GOT HOME from Gentian Hill Manor, the light was blinking on the answering machine. She set a sack of groceries on the kitchen counter, then listened to the message.

"Kate, this is Monica Mackenzie. You just left, but . . . I'd like to talk to you. Would you come horseback riding with me tomorrow morning? Give me a call. Thanks. Bye."

Kate checked her calendar. She had a Faith Freezer delivery scheduled at three in the afternoon, but her morning was free. Of course, Monica might intend to tell Kate to keep her nose out of their business, but she could easily have done that in a message. Kate prayed that Monica's call would be a friendly opening, then picked up the phone and dialed Gentian Hill Manor.

Paul came in a few minutes later. Kate was standing at the sink washing lettuce. He put his arms around her waist and kissed her neck. She giggled and turned her head to give him a kiss on the cheek.

"You were humming when I came in," he said. "You must have had a good day."

"I think I'm making progress."

"You think?"

"Uh-huh. Monica asked me to go riding tomorrow. She wants to talk to me."

Paul raised his eyebrows. "I'm not sure if that's positive or scary."

Kate laughed. "I know. I wondered that too. I went to see her this morning and took her a loaf of apple bread. She was polite but not exactly friendly, so I was surprised by her invitation."

"Must have been the bread. I hope you saved some for us."

"I did. How about a piece for dinner with a ham steak and collard greens?"

"*Mmm*. My mouth is watering. I'll clean up, then set the table." He started to walk away, then turned back. "I had lunch with Trace today."

"Well hurry back and tell me all about it. I want to hear what you talked about."

"I'll just say it was interesting. Be right back."

Kate made a face at his disappearing back. Just like him to drop a teaser, then leave her hanging, waiting to hear the rest. She just hoped it was all good news.

WHEN KATE AND MONICA entered the corral, the stable master came out leading two saddled horses. Monica took the reins of a beautiful palomino. She swung up into the saddle with practiced ease while the man led Rusty to a block so Kate could mount easily.

Kate scratched Rusty between the ears and rubbed his buttery-soft nose. He neighed, then softly blew into her hand. "Good boy," she said. She was glad to have the same horse again. This time Rusty didn't seem quite so large or intimidating.

"Are you up for a couple of hours' riding?" Monica asked. "I don't want to overdo it if you aren't used to riding."

"I'll be fine," Kate said. "But thanks for asking. My muscles have recovered from my ride with Jessica."

"It's easy to get saddle sore until you've ridden regularly for a while. We'll head toward town," she said.

Great, Kate thought, chuckling to herself. Everyone in town would see what a tenderfoot she was. She turned her horse and followed Monica out of the corral and up the driveway.

The fall colors had deepened since her ride with Jessica. A slight breeze rustled the branches overhead, sending deep red and blazing yellow leaves cascading around them as they ambled along down a gentle trail between the finger ridges toward the valley. Edged by colorful fall underbrush, the trail was only wide enough for one horse, so they plodded along, not talking, just enjoying the day.

The trail widened near the base, and Kate pulled alongside Monica. They came out east of the Hamilton Springs Hotel.

"I'm glad you could come along," Monica said.

Kate let out a silent sigh of relief. Monica's tone was open and devoid of hostility. "So am I. I used to ride when I was a kid. Several of my friends had horses. It's been a long time, though, except for last week with Jessica."

"You've gotten to know her well in a short time." Monica nodded.

"Yes. She's a special young woman," Kate said. "She reminds me of my daughters."

"Tell me about your children," Monica said.

"We have a son, Andrew. He's married with two children and lives in Philadelphia. Melissa lives in Atlanta with her family, and our youngest daughter, Rebecca, is a singer and actress in New York City."

"Are you close to your children?"

"Yes, very. We don't get to see them much, but we keep in touch every week thanks to telephones and the Internet."

"You're lucky."

"I'm very blessed," Kate said. "But I've had a lifetime to develop that closeness. I suspect it's not so easy when you come in at the middle."

Monica let out a humorless laugh. "For some reason, I can't seem to get this mothering business right. I mean, I know I'm not Jessica's mother, and I'm not trying to take Amelia's place, but Jess and I are like polite strangers. Well, sometimes I'm not always polite, I'm afraid . . . I don't try to be rude, but I know sometimes that's how I come off."

"I'm sure it can be difficult trying to mesh as a family." Kate really wanted to give Monica the benefit of the doubt. She leaned forward and rubbed Rusty's neck. "Was Jessica away at boarding school when you met Gordon?"

"Yes. And in those days, she was so involved with competition riding, her vacations revolved around meets and shows. We'd go, but I didn't know anything about horses then. They intimidated me. Since riding was something Gordon and Jessica shared, I was determined to overcome my fears and join in. I took lessons and forced myself to get my own horse and take care of her." Monica lovingly patted her horse's back. "Brian's father found Deoro for me in New Mexico. She was a raw one-year-old. Brian helped train her . . . and me. We have grown up together as horse and rider."

"Deoro, as in gold?"

Monica gave Kate a surprised look. "I'm impressed. Yes, I named her Niña de Oro, which basically means Golden Girl in Spanish. So I call her Deoro."

"She's beautiful."

Deoro blew out a little snort and nodded her golden head up and down, tossing her long mane. Monica leaned forward again and scratched her ears. "I should have named you *Niña Mimada*."

"Little spoiled girl?" Kate said, laughing.

Monica chuckled. "You really do know Spanish."

"*Poco. Muy poco*," Kate said, holding her thumb and forefinger close together to show how little she knew.

Monica laughed out loud, a joyous sound that startled Kate. "Me too," she admitted. She suddenly seemed younger and more carefree.

"I have a feeling we have a lot of things like that in common," Kate said, smiling.

Monica stopped Deoro and turned to look at Kate, her smile gone. Kate stopped her horse too. "Now you're being kind. I'm afraid I haven't been very nice to you."

"Nonsense. Although I am sorry that you felt uncomfortable around me. Honest, Monica, Jessica sees me as her friend and counselor, not a replacement for her mother."

Monica sighed. "I thought when she came home from boarding school that we'd be a family, but it didn't quite happen that way. Gordon said we should give her time to adjust. That was ten years ago and nothing's changed. She got more involved in school and riding, and when she did come home in the summer or on holidays, she and Gordon would go off together. I could see they needed time alone, so I didn't try to join them. Looking back, that was a mistake, but I just ..." Monica turned away and looked off at the wooded hillside. "I didn't fit in," she said in a quiet voice that drifted off into the trees. But Kate heard the hurt in her voice.

"When you saw Jessica in that dress, I saw in your expression just how much you care."

Monica turned back to Kate with a sad expression. "Isn't she gorgeous? She looks so much like her mother. Gordon's heart will break in two when he sees her. He still loves her, you know."

"Amelia?"

"Yes. Oh, he loves me too," Monica added when she saw Kate's confused expression. "I'm not jealous of his dead wife. He treats me like a queen and goes out of his way to make Gentian Hill Manor my home, letting me redo the colors, the decor, and the grounds. Those were all my ideas. He indulges me. But I'm so different from Jessica's mother, and I can't change who I am."

"Nor would Jessica want you to."

"I've been trying to get closer to Jessica with all this wedding stuff, but I just . . . I didn't realize how different our tastes were."

"I know she appreciates your help anyway, even when she gets frustrated." Kate's fingers curled tighter around the reins. "I think you two need a fresh start."

"I want that more than I can say. I don't know how, though." Monica's little laugh sounded like embarrassment. "This sounds juvenile, but I was wondering if maybe you could put in a good word for me?"

Kate's heart melted into a puddle at Monica's plea. "I don't know what I can do, but I'll do anything I can to help you. You're both missing out on so much."

"Thank you." Monica smiled. "Renee said you would help me. She respects you, I can tell, and she isn't afraid to tell me exactly what she thinks."

"That's our Renee," Kate said, grinning.

They'd reached the path along Copper Mill Creek. Birds were holding noisy conventions in the trees, gathering to prepare for the oncoming winter. Electric blue dragonflies darted among the low-growing plants along the creek. A cat hid among the grasses, waiting for unsuspecting prey. It looked up as they clopped past but apparently decided they weren't a threat and went back to its stakeout.

Along the way, Kate saw the path and bench that Gordon had donated as memorials to Jessica's mother. She knew

Monica must see those reminders of Gordon's first wife every time she came to town. They could be painful reminders, but she didn't seem to mind them.

As they passed the park and Main Street, then approached the end of Ashland Street, Kate looked down the road. Betty Anderson, owner of Betty's Beauty Parlor—also known as Copper Mill's very own gossip house—was getting into her car outside the pharmacy. Kate waved. Monica waved too. Betty shielded her eyes to see who it was. Kate could see a look of recognition—and surprise—on Betty's face. The bleached-blonde woman waved back, then drove off.

"I think we just provided the beauty shop with days' worth of gossip fodder."

Kate laughed. "You're probably right."

"I have a feeling my standing in town has just taken a turn for the better, thanks to you," Monica said. "Or yours will go down. After all, aren't we judged by the company we keep?"

"You and Gordon are loved in this town," Kate said. "So you've just done me more good than the other way around."

"Gordon and *Amelia* are loved. I'm still an outsider." Monica's tone held a touch of irony, but Kate detected a bit of sorrow as well.

"Amelia had a lot of friends in town, and Jessica's wedding has reminded them of her, but she's been gone a long time," Kate said. "I know you put on a lot of events for charity. Perhaps you could involve a few more local people."

"I don't know very many," Monica said. "We're gone most of the winter, and my friends are from Los Angeles or New Jersey, where I grew up."

"New Jersey? Isn't that where Anthony's from?"

Monica darted a surprised look at Kate. "Yes. How did you know that?"

"I overheard someone say it."

"Bertie, I bet. Poor man. I know he's jealous and feels like Anthony stole his job, but he can't keep up with a huge place like ours. I didn't tell him Anthony's older sister is one of my best friends from high school. They have a big family."

"Does he call them 'the family'?" Kate asked in a deep voice, attempting to imitate Flora with her poor rendition of a New Jersey accent.

Monica burst out laughing. "That's exactly what he calls them. And he lays it on thick. He loves playing the part, you know, the tough guy. It's a sham. He's totally harmless." Monica pulled the reins a little to the right, turning her horse a bit to the left. "You know he's footed the bill for all the landscaping?"

"I suspected as much," Kate said. "I saw him paying cash at the Mercantile. What I didn't know was why. How could he afford to do that?"

"He's become an established artist. He also ran a yard service way back when he was in junior high, mowing lawns and pruning bushes. The business grew from there. He went to Cornell and studied agriculture and horticulture on a full scholarship. His family owns a bakery, a pizza parlor, and a Laundromat, and his sister has a beauty shop. They've all invested in his art."

The clip-clop of the horses' feet on the hard-packed dirt was the only sound for a moment. "Gentian Hill Manor is his palette. He's doing the landscaping for the press. Magazines are fighting over the right to publish a story about his work at our home, and he's gotten a couple of offers for big projects out of it."

So Anthony was in it for the glory, not for the money. Kate was almost glad to hear it.

"I doubt we can keep him much longer," Monica continued. "He's making Gentian Hill Manor famous and gaining a great reputation. Brian is helping him with a business plan."

"Wow. That's quite a success story. Does Jessica know any of this?"

"I . . . I doubt it." Monica pulled up on the reins, stopping her horse. "She's close to Bertram and Florence. She and I have never really talked about the staff who came after them. Actually, we've never really talked about a lot of things."

Kate gave Monica an encouraging smile. "Such as?" She suspected she was finally getting to the real meaning of Monica's invitation to go riding.

"Trace, for one."

"Gordon doesn't want Jessica to marry Trace," Kate said.

"No, he doesn't." Monica shook her head. Her eyes looked sad.

"How do you feel about that?"

"I was totally on his side, but I'm not so sure anymore. I mean, Jessica seems to really love him. Is he a fortune hunter?" Monica reached out and patted her horse's mane. "I know some people said that about me, and I can't blame them. They don't know that the estate is already tied to Jessica. It came from her mother. It's all hers."

Kate couldn't help but be glad that Jessica would inherit the home she loved so much.

"That doesn't include all the resort properties, but a lot of that is just numbers on paper. Who knows what they're really worth?" She shrugged. "But then what if Trace is after her money? I don't want her to get hurt. And you know Brian adores her."

"That's pretty obvious."

"Poor guy. He's such a sweetheart. I've tried to get him to look at Kristin. She's got such a crush on him, but he's not interested." Monica sighed. "Why can't life be simple?"

"I suppose it would be easier on our hearts, but it would get pretty boring," Kate said.

"You amaze me," Monica said, laughing.

"Why's that?" Kate said.

"I expected a preacher's wife to be serious and pious and sort of tranquil. You're not at all like that."

Kate laughed. How often people had expectations of the clergy and their families. "I'm glad I don't fit the serious and pious mold. Tranquil? Well, I'm working on that."

"Don't work too hard. I like you like this."

"Thank you, Monica. I like you like this too."

SATURDAY AFTERNOON, Kate delivered orders of stained glass to some individual clients and one shop in Pine Ridge. As she got out of her car at the last stop, she noticed Kristin's red Mustang parked across the street at the same pawnshop she'd visited before. As much as Kate wanted to think more charitably toward Kristin, the girl's actions made it difficult.

Kate decided to catch her in the act. Instead of going into the gift store, she went across the street and entered the pawnshop.

Kate saw Kristin talking to the man at the counter, her hands gesturing emphatically. The girl didn't notice when Kate walked up behind her.

"Hello, Kristin," Kate said.

The young woman jumped and spun around, blocking the counter. "Kate! What are you doing here?" Kristin's eyes narrowed accusingly.

"I was across the street and saw your car, so I thought I'd stop in and say hi."

"Oh. Well, hi." She shifted nervously.

Kate looked past Kristin to the counter. The wide, bright red, stone-encrusted band stood out like a beacon. "How pretty. That looks a lot like Jessica's watch, actually. The one you were wearing the day Jessica had her wedding-dress fitting?"

Kristin gave Kate a defiant glare. "It's mine. She gave it to me. She doesn't like red."

"Oh. How strange. I could swear I heard her say that it was a gift from someone," Kate watched Kristin's eyes for a reaction.

"She doesn't want it anymore," Kristin muttered, looking away.

"Does this belong to you?" the man asked. He was the same man Kate had talked to the first time she went into the shop. He looked at Kate. "Do you have reason to believe this is stolen property?"

Kate kept her eyes on Kristin. "Jessica is very generous. She may have given Kristin the watch."

"She did. You can ask her. Here." Kristin punched in a number on her cell phone and put the phone up to Kate's ear.

Before Kate could object, Jessica answered.

"Hi, Jessica, it's Kate." She suddenly felt silly.

"Oh, Kate. I thought it was Kristin. Why are you calling from her number?"

"I'm on her cell phone. Uh . . . did you by chance give Kristin your red watch?"

"Yeah, I did. She was right. I don't wear red, and she loves bright colors. It'll look better on her anyway."

"Oh." Kate felt her cheeks flush. "I'm glad to hear that."

"She borrows things all the time, but she's never taken anything for good unless she's asked," Jessica added.

"Well, good. I'll let you get back to whatever you're doing."

Kate hung up and, with a rueful expression, handed the phone back to Kristin. "I'm sorry, Kristin. I jumped to the wrong conclusion."

"Yes, you did." Kristin picked up the watch off the counter and put it on. "I've decided to keep it," she said in a huff. She turned and left without saying another word.

Kate followed her out of the store, but Kristin got in her car and drove off.

Chapter Twenty

The pungent aromas of onions, cayenne, and ground beef told Kate that Paul was in the kitchen before she saw him stirring the contents of a large pot. The counter was strewn with empty cans, spice jar, smears of tomato sauce and chili powder. He was so preoccupied, he didn't hear her come in.

"Smells good in here. Shall I make corn bread to go with the chili?" she offered.

Paul stopped stirring and turned around. The lines of intense concentration across his brow eased as his mouth turned up in a chagrined smile. "I wasn't thinking about dinner, but corn bread sounds great."

"If not dinner, what's the occasion?"

"Oh, I just needed the mental exercise. I figured baking works for you, so I thought I'd give it a try. Only chili's my game." He got a dishrag to clean the counter.

"Is it working?"

Paul frowned. "No. But we'll have lots of chili."

Kate sat on a stool across the counter from him. "What's the problem? Maybe talking about it will open up your thoughts."

"I've still been struggling through writing the sermonette for Trace and Jessica's wedding ceremony. I can't seem to come up with the right words."

Kate nodded. "That's a tall order in this case. There's still too much distrust. Too many fractured relationships."

"Exactly. Although, Trace agreed to talk with Gordon about his finances, so hopefully that will make headway. Either way, I agreed to perform the wedding. I suppose I could use the bully pulpit to call them to set aside their distrust and unify, but that wouldn't be a good wedding message, and at least half the guests would wonder what's going on. On the other hand, I can't pretend the problems don't exist."

"If you didn't know about the strife between Jessica's family and Trace, what would you do?"

"Ignorance *would* be bliss in this case. Hypothetically, I'd perform a traditional ceremony, without anything personal."

"So it's your personal involvement with Jessica and Trace and Jessica's family that has you worried."

Paul stopped stirring for a second, looking thoughtful, then nodded.

"I'm having that same problem," Kate said. "To top it off, I'm trying to figure out who stole the money from Jessica's trust fund, and everyone around her seems suspect. I thought I'd found the culprit today, but then I discovered that I'd misjudged her cousin Kristin. I thought she'd stolen jewelry from Jessica and tried to sell it at the pawnshop in Pine Ridge. Turns out Jessica gave her the watch she was selling. I felt terrible when I discovered the truth."

"Did she accept your apology?"

"Not exactly. She ran off before I could explain. Also,

after the nice ride I had with Monica yesterday, it looks like I've misjudged her too."

"It's easy to jump to the wrong conclusions when you don't know the whole story."

Kate grimaced. "It's true. I've been too wrapped up in trying to catch the thief red-handed that I've ignored the complexities of each person's experiences." Kate shook her head, trying to cast off the self-chiding. "Gordon is the key, I think. If he would accept Trace, they could become a real family. Maybe if we could get to know him a little better, it would help."

"That sounds like good logic to me."

"I'm thinking of inviting Monica, Gordon, Jessica, and Trace here for dessert Monday night. What do you think?"

"I think it's a great idea," Paul said, lifting a spoonful of chili out of the pot. He blew on it, and wisps of steam rose into the air. "It might help smooth the way for Gordon and Trace. Good thinking, Katie."

"I'll ask." Kate motioned for Paul to bring the spoon closer to her, and she took a small bite of chili from the end. It was delicious. "Monica said something the other day that got me thinking. She said Gordon spent a lot of time with Jessica during her vacations, attending her equestrian meets. Monica encouraged them to be close, but the price she's paid is exclusion, I'm afraid. They haven't been a family of three. It's been Gordon and Monica, and Gordon and Jessica. They've never had a sense of family."

"Which would explain why Gordon's being so protective of Jessica."

Kate leaned back against the counter. "I guess that makes sense."

"As a father, I'd be concerned too. Jessica is impulsive. So he's hanging on to the report he got against Trace, although there were no charges or proof, because he's worried about his daughter," Paul said.

"I see your point," Kate said. "But none of this will help you with the wedding sermon."

"No, it sure won't." Paul tasted a bit of his chili. "Now that's good stuff."

Kate laughed. "You know, when you think of our wedding, our families rejoiced with us, and that made our day even more special. Becoming your wife meant everything in the world to me, but I had a sense that we were becoming part of something bigger than the two of us. Maybe thinking about our own story will help you write something about Jessica and Trace's."

"That's a good idea," Paul said.

"I remember worrying before Melissa and John's wedding that we were losing our daughter," Kate said. "She was starting her own family, and it would never be the same as having her in our home. Maybe Gordon is afraid he'll lose Jessica when she gets married."

"I remember feeling that too," Paul said.

"But we weren't losing a daughter at all," Kate said, smiling. "We simply became part of a larger family. It's like being part of the family of God. When love stretches, it doesn't break; it expands. Our finite minds have a hard time grasping that concept, and perhaps Gordon doesn't realize that God multiplies our love. It's never used up."

Paul's brow furrowed as he thought, and Kate noticed the tiny shift in roles that had occurred. Normally, Paul was the one reminding Kate of spiritual truths, but once in a while, she had an inspiration. That was part of being a couple—sharing burdens. She was more than happy to carry the load when her husband wasn't able to.

Paul lifted the pot lid and stirred absently. "I believe I can use that. I'm not sure how, but I think it'll work."

"If you want to go jot down some thoughts while the chili simmers, I'll watch it and make the corn bread," she offered.

"Great." He handed her the spoon and kissed her on the cheek. "Thanks. I'll just make a few notes."

Kate watched him walk out of the kitchen and across the living room to his study. He was whistling "To God Be the Glory."

Smiling, Kate gathered the ingredients and began mixing the corn bread.

While the bread baked, she picked up the phone to call Monica. She prayed Gordon would accept her invitation.

KATE SAT UP FRONT with the choir on Sunday morning. Looking out at the congregation, she was surprised to see an entire row taken up by the Mackenzie clan. Brian and Kristin sat next to each other, then Monica and Gordon. Jessica sat next to her father, with Trace on the other side.

After the singing, the choir filed down to the front pews, and Paul got up to speak. He welcomed the visitors, then launched into prayer and his sermon.

"My text today comes from Proverbs 3. Verses one through three say, 'My son, do not forget my teaching, but keep my commands in your heart, for they will prolong your life many years and bring you prosperity. Let love and faithfulness never leave you; bind them around your neck, write them on the tablet of your heart.'

"This, dear friends, is advice with a grand promise. The passage continues with verses four through six: 'Then you will win favor and a good name in the sight of God and man. Trust in the Lord with all your heart and lean not on your own understanding; in all your ways acknowledge him, and he will make your paths straight.'

"Too often," Paul said, "we trust our own wisdom. We think if we have an education, if we have experience, if we've lived a few years, we've gained wisdom. But our wisdom will fail. It'll let us down. Verses seven and eight say, 'Do not be wise in your own eyes; fear the Lord and shun evil. This will bring health to your body and nourishment to your bones.'"

Kate heard the sound of disturbance and murmured voices behind her. She resisted looking back. Her eyes on Paul, she saw him look up and pause for a few seconds before he continued reading.

"In Proverbs 4:20–22, it says, 'My son, pay attention to what I say; listen closely to my words. Do not let them out of your sight, keep them within your heart; for they are life to those who find them and health to a man's whole body.'"

Kate heard the back door open, then whoosh shut. She caught a flicker of distress in Paul's eyes, though she was sure no one else noticed.

"Wisdom and truth bring health," Paul continued.

Kate resisted the urge to look around to find out who was missing. It could have been a mother with a small child.

Sometimes people got up to get a drink or use the restroom. That flicker in Paul's eyes made her wonder, though.

Paul finished his sermon with the remaining verses in Proverbs 3. After his closing prayer, they sang a benediction, then the congregation filed out. Paul went to the front door to greet people as they left. Kate made her way to his side. He spoke to each parishioner by name, asking about his or her health or job or something that let the person know he took a personal interest in his parishioners' lives.

Paul and Kate greeted Monica and Kristin, but Gordon and Brian weren't with them. Kate glanced out to the parking lot and saw Brian and Gordon standing next to an SUV. She couldn't hear them, but the way they were standing, she thought they were having a serious discussion.

A few moments later, Kate saw Monica and Kristin join the men. She tried to remember what Paul had said that might have offended either of them.

Jessica and Trace hung back at the end of the line.

"Great sermon, Pastor," Trace said. "I remember a lot of proverbs from Sunday school. They're packed with good advice."

"It's true," Paul said. "So, did you get a chance to meet with Gordon last week?"

Trace shook his head. "I tried, but apparently he was out of town. I just asked him this morning. He didn't give me an answer. I'll try again this week. Please keep praying for me."

"Will do."

Jessica hugged Kate, and Trace shook Paul's hand, then the young couple left the church hand in hand.

As soon as they were gone, Kate turned to Paul. "What was the commotion in the middle of your sermon? Who left?"

"Gordon Mackenzie. He seemed to be in a hurry. I suppose you noticed that I lost my train of thought momentarily."

"I noticed, but no one else did. I thought you were disturbed about his leaving."

"I did wonder if I'd said something to upset him."

"Did Brian go out with him?"

Paul shook his head. "He followed a few minutes later, only he left a lot more quietly."

"I hope Gordon's okay." Kate tried to remember the last time she'd seen Gordon. Did he look especially tired or worn out?

"Maybe he just had heartburn . . . or my sermon was putting him to sleep."

"Never that," Kate said, smiling up at her husband.

Most people raved about Paul's preaching skills. Even so, on occasion an elderly parishioner would fall asleep. Then, loud snoring would rumble through the church, causing a ripple of laughter until someone woke the offender. Paul always took it in stride. He'd been preaching enough years to know the Holy Spirit worked under the best and the worst possible circumstances.

Chapter Twenty-One

Kate fluffed the pillows on the couch for the third time. The dinner dishes were done and put away. A pie was cooling on the counter, and the house smelled of caramelized butter, pecans, and fresh coffee. The doorbell rang.

"I'll get it," Paul said.

Kate went to the kitchen and put a cream pitcher and sugar bowl on a tray. The kettle whistled on the stove. She turned it off, then went to greet their guests.

"Welcome. I'm so glad you could come." She shook hands with Gordon, feeling grateful he'd accepted their invitation. Still, he looked stiff and leery. He sat at one end of the couch.

Jessica gave Kate a hug, then sat down beside Trace on the love seat. He took her hand and held on tightly.

"Can I help you get things ready?" Monica asked. Kate caught her pleading look.

"Yes, thanks. You can help me serve the pie and drinks."

Kate took orders for decaf coffee and tea, then she and Monica went to the kitchen.

"Thank you so much for inviting us over," Monica said quietly when they were in the kitchen. "Jessica and I had a little talk. I think we broke the ice, but we've got a long way to go. I'm worried about Gordon, though. This whole thing is starting to take a toll on him, I'm afraid."

"Is he ill?" Kate asked.

"I don't think so, but he seems . . . I don't know, moody. And I think he's having stomach problems. I see him every once in a while just pressing his hand against his stomach like it hurts. I'm concerned about him, but he says it's nothing. I'm worried it's an ulcer. I read up on ulcers, and they can be dangerous if not treated. Stress makes it worse, and he's extremely uptight over this wedding and Jessica's marriage to Trace."

"I've been praying for you and Gordon and Jessica. Maybe we can alleviate some of that stress tonight."

"I hope so. I'm praying too."

Kate cut the pie and put slices on plates while Monica added a scoop of vanilla ice cream. Then Kate poured three cups of coffee and three cups of tea.

When they'd served the group, Monica sat next to Gordon on the couch, and Kate took the empty chair, completing a circle around the coffee table.

"Would you mind if I ask a blessing on our time together?" Paul asked.

"Go ahead," Gordon said. He bowed his head, as did the others.

"Father, I thank you for bringing us together here tonight. Be with us, Lord, and fill us with your loving Spirit. Bless this wonderful smelling pie to nourish us, and bless our fellowship together. In Jesus' name. Amen."

"Amen," Trace added.

It was silent for a moment, then there was a clink of metal forks against china plates.

"Delicious pie," Gordon said. "Nothing in the world like good ol' Southern pecan pie."

"How about mid-Texas pecan pie," Kate replied with her deepest drawl. She raised her eyebrows.

Gordon chuckled. "How could I miss that accent? I concede. Texas pecan pie is every bit as good as Southern Tennessee pie." He seemed to relax then, which was exactly what Kate wanted. He set his empty plate on the coffee table and took hold of Monica's hand.

"Kate's one of the best cooks in the county," Paul said. "We've had a lot of special gatherings around her cooking."

"Yeah, they're called family dinners," Kate joked.

"I mess around in the kitchen a little, but I've never mastered pie crust," Monica said.

"There are a few tricks. Mostly it takes practice," Kate offered.

"I'll stick to the frozen pies at the Mercantile," Jessica said.

"I love chess pie from the Country Diner," Trace said. "Reminds me of my mom's custard pie, but richer."

It was the first comment he'd made since he'd added an "amen" to Paul's prayer. Gordon gave him a sharp glance but didn't say anything. Jessica's smile dimmed.

"I understand you spend quite a bit of time at your resorts these days," Paul said, setting down his empty plate and looking at Gordon. "Will you be heading out again after the wedding?"

"Yes. We'll be spending most of the winter in Hawaii."

"It's so beautiful there," Jessica said wistfully. She glanced at Trace. "I love riding in the hills around the resort. It's so lush, and there are miles of beaches."

"It's a beautiful setting, but I won't be sorry to see it go," Gordon said. "I'm getting too old for all this travel."

Jessica turned a wide-eyed gaze on her father. "I didn't know you're selling Ho'okipa Shores." She turned toward Trace. "My grandfather built the resort before I was born. It's so beautiful there, and it holds so many memories. I'm glad we get to go there for our honeymoon before it's too late."

"It must take a tremendous amount of work to keep a resort up to date and in good repair," Paul said.

"Too much work," Gordon said. "Keeping good staff is a challenge too. Eventually I hope to pare down to one or two resorts. Then maybe we can spend more time in Copper Mill. Monica has talked about spending more time here ever since I met her." He squeezed her hand.

Gordon stared at Jessica and Trace's entwined hands and frowned. Then he looked down at Monica's hand in his, and his frown eased. He turned to Paul. "I've got a threesome for golf Thursday afternoon. Would you like to join us?"

Paul barely blinked, though Kate was surprised by Gordon's invitation.

"I'd like that," Paul said, a bit concerned that Gordon was excluding Trace. "But I'd hate to slow you down."

"It's no problem," Gordon persisted. "We're not in any hurry. Monica has a crew coming in to work on the patio for the . . . for the wedding." He glanced at Monica. "I figure that's a good time to make myself scarce."

"Smart man. Yes, then. Thank you," Paul said, then glanced at Trace, who seemed not to be offended.

Monica glanced at Jessica, then Kate. "The preparations are coming together nicely, I think."

Jessica nodded. "We're working it out."

"There's one detail that hasn't been taken care of," Trace said, looking at Gordon. "Maybe this is the time . . ."

Gordon frowned. "What do you mean?"

Trace cleared his throat and sat forward on the edge of the love seat. "Sir, I never formally asked you for your daughter's hand in marriage. We'd really like your blessing."

"Please, Daddy," Jessica said, giving her father a pleading look. She turned to her stepmother. "And Monica. We want you both to be happy for us."

Kate saw Monica's hand tense on her coffee cup. She was watching Gordon for his reaction.

Gordon took a deep breath, sitting up to his full height. His face reddened. Kate began to worry that he might be building up to a heart attack or something. She looked at Paul. He was watching Gordon too.

"I do appreciate your asking," Gordon said. "But it's a little too late. You should have come to me before you asked my daughter and got her hopes up."

"Daddy—"

"I understand you found out that I looked into your background," he told Trace, cutting Jessica off.

"Yes sir. I heard that."

"You were accused of mishandling funds from a bank where you worked."

Trace's gaze never wavered from Gordon's. "I wasn't charged with any crime, sir."

Gordon's hard look didn't waver. "You were lucky they didn't press charges."

"What happened at the bank was the result of an encoding error. It's true it cost the bank a great deal of money, but I accepted full responsibility."

"An encoding error?" Gordon shook his head. "You expect me to believe that? I know you graduated summa cum laude. You're supposed to be an IT expert. You're no doubt capable of decoding any kind of bank transactions or accounts and moving funds around."

"Daddy!" Jessica jumped to her feet. "Trace never did anything like that."

Gordon's voice rose. "Jessica, you trust people too easily." He glared at Trace. "You could do all that, couldn't you? You have the ability, don't you?"

Trace sighed. "If I was dishonest, I could have hacked into accounts that didn't belong to me, but I'm not dishonest. Mr. Mackenzie, I did not steal money from anyone." Trace paused. "Sir," he continued, his voice steady, "I have files of financial records I'm willing to share with you. And I've already told Jessica I'd sign a prenuptial agreement. I want to earn your trust."

"That's all fine and good, Trace," Gordon said, "but what about the bank? Can you prove to me you were innocent there? How do I know you didn't steal Jessica's money? Or that you're not after mine?"

Trace didn't speak; he just set his elbows on his knees and rested his chin on his hands.

"Gordon." Monica's voice was soft and pleading. "A lot of people thought that about me, but you trusted me."

"That's different. I know you."

"Jessica's your daughter. She inherited your kindness and generosity. Why can't you believe she also inherited some of your perceptiveness?"

Kate couldn't help but inwardly beam at Monica's standing up for Jessica and Trace. Gordon, however, didn't seem convinced.

"I can't take that chance," he said. "I can't stand to see her throw away her life." Gordon stood. "I'm sorry, Jessica. You insist on this marriage, and you're an adult, so I can't stop you. But unless you can prove your trustworthiness, Trace, I can't give you my blessing. Monica, we've got to go."

He turned to Kate. "Thank you for the pie." He turned to Paul and gave him a brief nod. "Thank you for your hospitality. I'll see you on Thursday?"

"I'll be there," Paul said, standing. Kate noticed him trying to give Gordon a genial look, though his brow was wrinkled with concern.

Monica gave Jessica and Trace an apologetic look, then turned to Kate. Kate gave her a brief hug and whispered, "Keep praying."

Monica nodded and then followed Gordon to the door. Paul saw them out.

Jessica buried her head against Trace's shoulder and wept. He wrapped his arms around her and held her. She lifted her head and wiped her eyes.

"Isn't there anything you can say to convince him?" she asked Trace.

He shook his head. "I'm sorry, honey. I'd give anything to help mend this rift between you and your father."

"He'll come around. Someday, I hope. And I think Monica's coming around. Maybe she can convince him."

Kate wanted to shake some sense into Gordon Mackenzie and make him see the misery he was causing his daughter and himself. She was more determined than ever to find the thief who stole Jessica's trust fund.

KATE RAN ERRANDS early Tuesday morning. She got home in time for the FedEx delivery of supplies she'd ordered for her stained-glass projects. A large flat box contained a brass fire-place screen for a special order. Kate couldn't wait to begin the project.

She was unpacking one of the boxes when the doorbell rang. Monica was at the door. She was wearing a workout suit and no makeup. Her hair was pulled back in a big clip, with ends sticking out all over. Kate was surprised. Even when they'd gone riding and when she'd seen Monica gardening, she'd looked put together, like part of a fashion magazine spread.

"Monica, hi. Is anything wrong?"

"I'm sorry to bother you, Kate."

"No bother. I was just working in my studio. What's up?"

"I need to talk to you about the wedding. Some plans have changed. I could talk to Renee, but I fear she would be too discouraged."

"Oh?" Kate's first thought was that the wedding was off, but she discarded that concern. Trace and Jessica were deter-mined to get married, and they had family and friends com-ing from long distances. "Come on into the kitchen."

"I don't want to disrupt your work. I just need to bounce

some things off of you, if you don't mind. I can talk while you work," Monica said.

Kate liked to work alone, without distractions, but she showed Monica into her studio anyway. Monica looked around. The room was neat. Kate always put her tools and supplies away. Several Christmas ornaments sat on the light table.

"May I pick them up?" Monica asked.

"Yes. They're finished."

Monica reached out for a frosted-glass angel holding a gold horn. "A herald angel?" she asked.

"Yes. I make all kinds of designs, but I love the ones that represent the spiritual side of life."

"You do lovely work," Monica said, looking around at the few samples Kate had out. She saw the screen on Kate's work-table. "Is that a fireplace screen? Are you making stained-glass panels for it?"

"It's a special order. It's the only large order I'm accepting for Christmas. The customer wants a nativity scene to put in front of an electric fireplace." Kate showed Monica her sketches. "The nativity will take up the center panel, with Mary and Joseph and baby Jesus at the bottom in bright jewel tones, and a cross and herald angels above. The side panels will have shepherds on one side and the wise men on the other."

"Wow. That sounds like a museum piece."

Kate laughed. "It won't be quite that elaborate. I'm very excited about it, though."

"I want to see it when it's finished, and maybe order a screen for the house. I saw your window at the church. I enjoyed the service too. Maybe we'll come again. At least

I might come with Jessica and Trace." She bit her lip. "I don't know if Gordon will come."

"I hope he's all right."

"Well . . ." Monica let out a breath. "This morning we got a call from Henry Balderson. The trustee of the estate?" Kate nodded. "Apparently, the Mid-Cumberland Bank and Trust notified him that another bank was looking into Jessica's financial accounts."

Kate raised her eyebrows. "How so?"

"Well, Henry didn't know all the details because, as he put it, some Mid-Cumberland employees 'aren't the freshest bills in the bundle.' But according to Henry, someone in Copper Mill has gotten into Jessica's banking records." Monica looked at Kate and hesitated before she spoke again. "All it took was a phone call to find out the name of the person who initiated the inquiry."

"Oh no. Please tell me it's not . . ." Kate slumped down in her chair.

"Trace Jackson." Monica turned the stained-glass angel in her hand. "Gordon is livid."

"But how did they track that information down?" Kate put her elbow on her worktable and held her head in her hand.

"All Henry knows is that Trace's bank contacted Mid-Cumberland and requested the details of Jessica's accounts." Monica handed the stained-glass angel to Kate, who set it on her worktable. "Apparently, they wanted information not only about her trust fund, but also about her other accounts, investments, etcetera. Henry said that he's going to get to the bottom of this, but in the meantime . . . Gordon has pulled the funding for the wedding."

"Oh no." Kate shook her head. "There has to be a mistake. Trace wouldn't . . ."

Kate couldn't finish her sentence. She wanted to trust Trace, but he *had* just admitted the night before that he could hack into banking software. And surely Henry Balderson wouldn't have been notified unless it was true.

"Gordon's refusing to shell out any more money for what he calls a farce of a marriage," Monica said. She sighed and sat on the chair on the far side of the worktable.

"Poor Jessica," Kate murmured.

"Well, I haven't told her the whole story, just that Gordon is shrinking the budget because he thinks it's gotten out of hand. Jessica didn't seem to mind"—Monica chuckled dryly— "in fact, she seemed to agree. That girl has no concept of entertaining well. But I couldn't tell her about the bank records and add to her distress. How is she going to handle learning that her fiancé has even more suspicion cast on him now?" She shook her head with resolve.

"I even convinced Gordon to wait until Henry sends us more solid information before he confronts Trace. Gordon said himself last night that Trace is really smart. Why would he do something that looks so incriminating when he'll have access to Jessica's money after the wedding?" Monica shook her head.

"There must be a logical explanation," Kate said, her mind puzzling through this new conundrum. She couldn't believe Trace would be so brazen.

"I agree. Besides, we can't call off the wedding. Only Jessica can do that, and I doubt she will." Monica sighed. "So for now, I've started making adjustments to the plans. I called this morning and canceled the flowers. I can't cancel the dinner. That's a must. We have all those out-of-town guests, and they have to eat, but I called the Bristol, and I can substitute chicken for the pheasant and save a bunch. It will be a stretch, but I think I can cover it."

"Do you mean . . ."

"I have a little money of my own, and if Jessica's intent on going through with the wedding, I'm going to do whatever I can to make this day special for her."

Kate was thankful for Monica's new attitude toward her stepdaughter. "I'll do whatever I can to help too. Let's see . . . If I remember right, you had prime rib and salmon on the menu, and you had appetizers. Maybe you could—"

"Well, not anymore. I hate to cut the hors d'oeuvres, but I don't see a choice. That would cut down on food and servers."

"I have an idea. Why don't you ask Flora about her tea treats? She has some marvelous ideas for finger foods. I bet she'd love to help you."

"Flora?" Monica frowned. "She doesn't like me very much, I'm afraid."

"I don't know about that, but she loves Jessica, and I think she'd do anything to help her."

"I guess I could ask. I'm willing to try anything at this point." Monica combed her fingers through her messy hair. "I wish there were some way to have flowers too."

"Have you ever been to Flora's cottage?"

"No." Monica shook her head. "I haven't."

"What do you say we pay her a visit?"

Chapter Twenty-Two

I know Gordon is just doing what he thinks is best for his daughter," Monica said as they drove down Mountain Laurel Road. "He thinks Trace will end up betraying her, and right now, I can totally see his point. Things don't look good for Trace. The bank incident in Virginia was bad enough. Now that he's made inquiries into Jessica's account . . . it just doesn't add up. I want to trust him, and because I want to honor Jessica—and to make up for some of our past struggles—I will try." Monica idly tapped the steering wheel. "But Gordon has a right to be concerned."

"The more I think about it, the more I'm certain there's a logical explanation," Kate said. She was pretty sure the bank inquiry was part of Trace buying the house for Jessica. After all, her name would have to be on the mortgage. But she couldn't tell Monica and spoil Trace's surprise. She sighed. "They're preparing to start a life together. We've discussed finances in our premarital counseling sessions, and they've both been very thoughtful in preparing their budget. Maybe they applied for a joint credit card."

Monica shot a startled glance at Kate. "Of course. I never thought of that. Makes perfect sense." She exhaled a sigh of relief. "Thanks Kate. I'll mention that to Gordon. He doesn't need more worry right not. He has enough to worry about with the resorts lately. Running seven resorts takes a lot of time and energy. We have good managers, but it's a constant juggling act."

Monica pushed a wayward strand of hair behind her ear. "It's just all too much. I wish he'd never invested in foreign resorts. He and Brian bought two, and since then, his stress level has shot out into the ozone. He worries about power and weather and unstable governments." Monica shook her head. "It's just crazy. I wish he'd stuck with investing in horses. That's risky enough."

"I saw Brian's ranch on the Internet," Kate said as Monica made a smooth right turn onto Sweetwater Street. "It looks like a beautiful place."

"It is beautiful. Very different from here. It's dry, rugged country. But you're from Texas, so you know what it's like."

"Brian and his father raise racehorses. I imagine that's a speculative business."

"Sure is. You never know how a horse will show, even with championship bloodlines. I love the horses but not the business. I'm trying to convince Gordon to bring Fleetfoot's colts here to train."

Kate remembered seeing the beautiful stallion online. "Won't they be trained for racing? They must be very valuable."

"No, there's a genetic problem with them. Brian won't keep them at the ranch because they're worth almost nothing. I suggested donating them to New Providence Ranch. It's a rehabilitation ranch for people with injuries and disabilities, but they have to be broken and trained first. I don't know what their other options are."

"What about Fleetfoot? What will happen to him?"

"I don't know. He's a good horse, but they can't race him or use him for stud. It's too bad. I'd love to breed him with Deoro. The foals would be beautiful." She shrugged. "But Gordon says we can't take a chance."

Kate told her where to turn, and they pulled into the treed driveway to the Ripples' cottage. Kate waited for Monica's reaction. She wasn't disappointed.

"Wow! This place is gorgeous. Bertie transplanted all the roses and bushes from the estate here, didn't he?"

"Aren't they fabulous?"

Monica parked, and they got out of the car. She stood in front of the cottage looking around. "I feel like I've been transported to Stratford-upon-Avon," she said. "Gordon took me to the horse races there a couple of years ago. Not my style, but it's beautiful."

"You'll have to tell that to Flora and Bertie."

"Of course. They're both from England, aren't they?"

"Yes. And they've re-created a bit of England here." Kate went up to the door and rang the bell. The ring sounded like Westminster chimes. She heard the shuffle of feet, then Flora opened the door.

"Hello, Kate. Who did you bring to see me?" She opened the screen door and peered out. "Monica! Well, I never expected to see you here."

"May I come in?" Monica asked.

"Well, now, I am a properly bred Englishwoman. Can't say

why you'd be wanting to come in, but you're welcome." Flora shot a questioning glance at Kate.

"I brought you some of Paul's homemade chili. I hope you like it," she said, handing the container to Flora.

Flora accepted it, smiling. "Lovely. Bertie and I will have it for supper." She stood aside. "Come in."

"Thank you. We came here because we need your advice," Kate said, moving into the front room.

Flora's hand went to her chest. "My advice?" She glanced at Monica. "How peculiar." She led them to the parlor and bade them sit down. The chairs were covered in rose chintz.

"Kate suggested . . . ," Monica said, then stopped. "I know you don't have much use for me, and I can't blame you, but I need your help for Jessica's sake."

Flora straightened up. "Jessica? What's wrong with my girl?"

"She's fine. It's her wedding. But I'm afraid we need to cut the budget back a bit, and Kate thought you could help. She's raved about your cooking and the hors d'oeuvres you serve with tea. I wanted to serve finger foods during the reception before the dinner, but I don't have the budget for them now."

"Ah." Flora nodded to Kate, then turned back to Monica. "You've come to the right place. Jessica loves my tea parties."

"I'd planned to serve sparkling punch, but we could have tea available."

"If it's pennies you're pinching, you can have fruit-tea punch, either hot or cold, depending on the weather. Save the sparkling juice for a toast to the bride and groom. Then you don't need to buy as much. We'll serve low tea."

"I thought it was high tea," Monica said.

"No, no. That's a meal in itself, served at the high table, or the dining room. Low tea is a midday snack with finger foods and delicacies. Isn't that more what you'd be wanting?"

"Yes," Monica said, although she didn't look too sure.

Kate almost chuckled but refrained. Poor Monica no doubt wondered if she'd made a mistake coming to Kate and now Flora.

"I'm thinking a bit of rarebit and toast, dipped fruit, asparagus rolls, and crème brouchées," Flora said.

Kate noticed Monica's wide-eyed look. For all the traveling she'd done, the woman was obviously unfamiliar with English tea parties.

"Your watercress sandwiches are wonderful. Do you have enough?" Kate asked, knowing full well she was teasing Monica even more.

"I have a bumper crop."

Monica's expression caught Flora's attention. "No doubt you're wondering if you've fallen down Alice's rabbit hole. Come tomorrow afternoon for tea. You can taste some of my dainties. Then you can decide. I'll need helpers, and we'll have to rush order the ingredients, so we've no time to waste. Kate, you'll come too."

Kate thought about her day. She had a lot of work to do, but she couldn't leave Monica alone to cope with Flora, not until they got to know each other better. "All right."

"I'll pick you up on the way," Monica said. "May I bring Renee? She's been such a huge help in planning the wedding."

Flora nodded graciously.

"Thank you, Florence," Monica said.

"Sounds wonderful," Kate said. "Mind if I show Monica around your gardens?" she asked.

Flora perked up. "Come along. I'll show you." Flora took them out through the kitchen. Kate noticed the Dresden figurines were gone, replaced by a stunning Lalique amber vase surrounded by vines and faces in relief. Kate wondered if it would appear on eBay soon.

They stepped out the back door into the lush garden.

"If the weather permits, we'll take tea out here," Flora said.

"So now I know what Bertram did with all the roses," Monica said.

"It's Bertie, darling. And you can call me Flora."

Monica's face blushed as she nodded. Kate suppressed a smile, glad for Flora's welcoming gesture.

"Anyway," Flora continued, "you were going to throw all those roses away," she said, a bit defensive.

"Oh, well . . . I'm glad they're here. They're beautiful."

Flora gave her a sharp look, as if she wasn't sure whether to believe her. "I'm glad to hear you say that."

"How do you keep the roses blooming so late in the year?" Monica asked.

"Proper care and a gentle touch," Flora said. "Bertie knows his roses."

"I can see that."

After a quick tour, Kate and Monica left.

"I have to admit, I never expected help from Flora," Monica said as she drove toward town.

Kate chuckled. "Wait until you taste her scones and dainties, as she calls them. By the way, I told you I had an idea about your flowers."

Monica glanced over at her. A lightbulb seemed to switch on. "Roses . . . Jessica said she wanted them. Are you thinking of Bertie's roses?"

"Yes. Can you think of anything more fitting? Bertie adores Jessica, and they were her mother's rosebushes. You wouldn't mind that, would you?"

"I think it's a fabulous idea," Monica said, smiling wider than Kate had seen all day. "If Bertie will agree."

"I'll be very surprised if he doesn't offer first."

TUESDAY NIGHT, Trace and Jessica met with Paul and Kate for their final premarital counseling session. They spent the time discussing intimacy and meeting each other's emotional needs.

As the session wrapped up, Paul asked, "So, how are the wedding preparations going?"

Jessica groaned. "You know Daddy's not paying for the wedding anymore. But I don't care about that. All we care about is getting married, with our families and friends there to celebrate with us. I just wish . . ." She turned toward Trace.

Kate was glad Jessica didn't know about the bank-record news. She worried what it would do to Trace and Jessica's dwindling hope of a reconciliation with Gordon. When she caught Paul's eye, she knew he was thinking the same thing.

"We wish Jessica's father felt differently," Trace said, "but I don't know what else to do to convince him how much I love his daughter."

"I know one more thing we can do," Paul said, leaning forward in his chair. "We can pray." The young couple nodded, so Paul and Kate joined hands with Jessica and Trace as Paul prayed for them, for their marriage, and for their families.

After Trace and Jessica left, Paul turned off the lights and locked up the church. "Well, they're in God's hands now. But then, they always were."

Kate put her hand through the crook of Paul's arm. "Yes. And that's the best place they could be."

"Now if I could just come up with the wedding sermonette."

She looked up at him, getting a flashback of him officiating at their daughter's wedding. He'd been so handsome in his tuxedo. When he'd addressed the couple and the guests, his words had been so beautiful and heartfelt, most of the women had dabbed at their eyes. "You're still struggling with it?"

"'Fraid so. My thoughts still won't gel."

"I'm sorry. I know God will give you the perfect message at just the right time, and you'll deliver it with eloquence."

He opened the truck door for her, then planted a kiss on her forehead before she climbed in. "I appreciate your confidence, Katie girl, and I know you're right that the Lord will come through, but sooner rather than later would be good."

Chapter Twenty-Three

Kate wanted to spend time Wednesday morning on the stained-glass fireplace screen, since tea at Flora's was sure to take up a good part of the afternoon. She started to set up her studio, but she couldn't get the puzzle of Jessica's missing money and Gordon's distrust of Trace out of her mind.

Then she thought of Monica's concern for Gordon. What was going on with him? Was he suffering from ill health, as Monica suspected? Kate even wondered if he could be experiencing financial difficulties, but that seemed improbable for such a wealthy man. Still, he was selling off some resorts. Maybe business wasn't as good as he made it out to be?

Unable to concentrate, she put her supplies away and headed for the library.

She said hello to Livvy and then went upstairs and checked her e-mail first as she did every time she logged on, hoping for some contact from Art Franklin. Still nothing. Discouraged, she answered a few personal e-mails, deleted the spam, then went on the Web. She returned to the Arroyo Robles Thoroughbred Ranch Web site and looked up Fleetfoot Mac. His picture had been removed.

She looked at the foals and one-year-olds for sale. None were sired by Fleetfoot. Monica had mentioned a genetic problem. That horse alone could have cost Gordon a fortune. He'd won several races and placed in others, so Gordon had recouped some of his expenses, but as an investment, the horse now seemed to be a liability.

Kate remembered from her earlier research that a good sire brought anywhere from two hundred thousand to five hundred thousand dollars for a one-year-old colt. She supposed the horse was insured, but Gordon must have been disappointed at the least. Since Fleetfoot was bred to Brian's mares, Brian must have lost hundreds of thousands of potential dollars on the colts. She doubted that loss would be insured. Could Brian be having financial troubles as well? He had access to Gordon's office. He could have gone through Gordon's files or searched his computer to learn how to get into Jessica's trust fund.

Still, the ailing racehorse didn't seem like the reason for Gordon to be in trouble. From what Kate understood, the vacation properties were his primary business. Kate searched online for Mackenzie Resorts. On the home page, a slide show scrolled through enticing pictures of sunny beaches, lush golf courses, pristine pools, and snowy ski runs. As she clicked on the different pages, she found everything from luxury hotel rooms to cozy condominiums and cabins in Colorado, New Mexico, California, Hawaii, and Florida.

The resorts looked fabulous, and the five-star ratings and glowing customer reviews led Kate to conclude the Mackenzie fortune must be even more vast than she'd imagined. She envisioned vacationing with Paul at one of the locations.

She remembered Monica and Renee looking at fabrics for a resort in the Colorado mountains. She went to the site for the Telluride resort. It looked like any hotel or resort in a ski town might look. She scrolled through several reviews of the resort. Two of them mentioned shabby conditions or old appliances, but the services were rated well. Monica had said the units needed remodeling. Kate had thought she meant a change in decor, but these reviews indicated more than upgrading curtains and carpets.

Kate couldn't imagine the work of keeping up one resort property, let alone seven! The Mackenzie fortune went back at least a generation, so Kate figured that some of the resorts must be old. Still, she assumed that remodeling would be part of the regular maintenance.

Kate followed links to businesses near the various resorts. Arroyo Robles Thoroughbred Ranch was listed near the Mackenzie's New Mexico property.

At the bottom of the resort-listings page, Kate found a link to "More Resort Properties." Why would Gordon advertise other resorts? Unless . . .

Kate remembered Monica's comment that Gordon and Brian had invested in foreign properties. She clicked on the link, which brought up two resorts, both overseas. One was on the island of Fiji. The other was on a private island near Bali. M and L Partnership owned the properties. That could stand for Mackenzie and Levy, Kate surmised. The resort in Fiji showed palm trees and flowering orchids and a colorful sailboat on a glassy lagoon. She clicked on the resort near Bali. A blank page came up with the words *Under Construction*.

Did that mean the resort or the Web page? Perhaps Gordon and Brian were in the middle of a building project.

Kate hadn't reached any conclusions about Brian or Gordon, but either way, the prognosis was not good.

COPPER MILL WAS EXPERIENCING a spell of Indian summer, and the afternoon sun warmed Flora's backyard, bringing out the scents of roses, raspberry-tinged pink and purple chalices, and a profusion of asters and chrysanthemums. The round table in the gazebo was set with a pale peach linen tablecloth and matching cloth napkins. A huge yellow rose unfurled its petals in a round crystal bowl in the center of the table.

"This is simply gorgeous," Renee said as she fluttered her fingers and looked around. "It's as if I've landed in the British Isles."

"Beautiful, isn't it?" Monica said.

Flora had insisted they sit at the table while she waited on them. Kate had to smile. She knew the former housekeeper was in her element as hostess, showing off her home and her beloved ritual of afternoon tea.

Flora came out of the house carrying a black lacquered tray. She set it down. The fine china tea set depicted a fruit motif with apples, pears, grapes, strawberries, and cherries. Kate hadn't seen the set before and wondered if it was part of Florabunda's Attic inventory, but she didn't ask.

Bertie helped Flora carry out the goodies and another teapot. Kate recognized the cabbage-rose pattern from before. They heard a car pull into the driveway. A moment later, Jessica came around the house.

"Hi. Oh good, I made it." She gave Flora and Bertie hugs, then pulled up a chair next to Kate. Kate noticed Monica's sheepish look and surmised that she hadn't yet told Jessica about the bank-records incident.

"I've looked forward to this all day," Jessica said as she eyed the array of goodies. "Flora, you've outdone yourself. This is a feast! I won't need dinner tonight."

"Nor will I, because I intend to taste one of everything," Renee said. "Mother will have to fend for herself." Kate could only chuckle. Renee and her mother, Caroline, always seemed to be at odds.

Flora served miniature quiches; meat tarts; asparagus bundles; dipped fruits; watercress, chicken, and deviled-ham sandwiches; scones; handmade butter mints; and truffles.

Bertie set a platter down and started to walk away.

"You're going to join us, aren't you, Bertie?" Jessica asked.

"I . . ." He eyed the food. "If you don't mind?" he said, looking at Monica.

"Please do," she said.

Bertie pulled up another chair and sat.

"We have Earl Grey tea and a mango black tea. Which would you prefer?" Flora asked as she began to pour. When everyone had a cup, she passed a plate of scones.

"Jessica can tell you how to prepare your scones," Flora said as she passed a plate of large strawberries, banana bites, cherries, and apricots dipped in chocolate. Next she passed little, savory, bite-size tarts.

"This is spectacular," Renee said. "And you know how to make a good cup of tea." She gave Kate a superior look. "You really should open a tea shop in town, dear."

Flora's face brightened with pleasure. "If I were ten years younger, I might just do that, but I enjoy my retirement too much to take on such an enterprise." She winked at Kate. "I manage quite well with our eBay business. I acquired this tea set at an estate yard sale, and I'll put it up on eBay when the time is right."

"These hors d'oeuvres will be perfect for the wedding reception," Monica said, biting into a miniquiche. "I've never tasted such a flaky crust before."

"I can whip up a whole bunch of those," Flora said. "Just let me know how many you need."

"There's one other item for the wedding that needs attention," Kate said, giving Bertie a meaningful look, hoping he'd be alert to the conversation. Then she looked at Monica and tilted her head toward the gardens.

"Oh yes," Monica said, taking the hint. "I've had to cancel the order of tropical flowers. It's too costly to import them from Hawaii. Besides, Jessica has her heart set on roses."

Jessica blinked as if shocked at Monica's announcement. "W-we don't have to have a lot of flowers," she said.

"Hold up there," Bertie said. "I'll be pruning these roses and transplanting some in a couple of weeks. You can have all the roses you want. I'll personally cut and deliver them. How's that?"

"Oh, Bertie!" Jessica jumped up and hugged the gardener. "That'd be perfect! Wouldn't it, Monica?"

"Yes," Monica sneaked a glance at Kate and then looked back to Bertie. "Thank you, Bertie. You're very generous."

Bertie blushed and looked very pleased. "They're your roses . . . or they were."

"No. They're your roses. You saved them, and I'm glad you did. This is the perfect setting for them," Monica said. "We'll need to get vases."

"I have two dozen square, leaded glass vases in the shop," Flora said. "They're part of our inventory that I purchased as overstock. You can use them, then I'll sell them later. I plan to decorate them with greens for Christmas and sell them at the Christmas Craft Extravaganza in town."

"Wonderful," Monica said. "Perhaps we could use some of the more open blooms in bowls on the dinner tables, like you've done here. It makes a lovely table centerpiece. Simple and elegant."

"I'm so excited," Jessica said. "This is perfect. Just the way I envisioned my wedding."

Kate couldn't rejoice in the circumstances that caused Gordon to cut the budget for the wedding, but she could be thankful that they had brought Monica and Jessica closer together. *Thank you, Lord,* Kate thought. God promised to work all things for the good of those who loved him. She could see his hand at work, and it delighted her.

FRIDAY WAS HALLOWEEN. The youth department at Faith Briar Church had planned a fall festival and invited the community, so Kate had promised to make six dozen cupcakes. By nine thirty that morning, they were out of the oven and spread out on the counter to cool. Kate was mixing dark fudge frosting when her phone rang.

"Kate, it's Monica. Any chance you can come by the house this morning? I need your help."

"I'm in the middle of frosting cupcakes. What time?"

"Would eleven work?"

Kate thought about her day. She had laundry to do, but Monica and Gordon would be leaving for Hawaii for the winter after the wedding, so her time to deepen her relationship with Monica was growing short. Plus, Kate would take just about any excuse to procrastinate on laundry.

"I can make it."

"Great. I'll see you then."

Kate hung up and went back to mixing the frosting. She decorated the tops with candy corn and piped orange pumpkins. Satisfied, she went to change. Maybe today she could learn something more about Gordon and Brian's business partnership.

The thought had nagged at Kate since her Internet research the other day: Brian seemed like Prince Charming, but was he a villain in disguise?

"THANKS FOR TAKING THE TIME to help me," Monica said as Kate walked beside her at the Mackenzie mansion. "I know you're busy, and we've monopolized a lot of your schedule lately. But," she said with a grin, "I want you to see the wedding program I've created on Gordon's computer. It's in his office at the stables. Before I send it to the printer, I'd like a second opinion." She led Kate through the house to the back door. "And I want to thank you for taking me to see Flora and having Bertie offer the roses."

"You're welcome. I think they're thrilled to help."

"I know Jessica's pleased. And I noticed how you got it to be their idea. I think maybe I'm not the enemy anymore."

"I hope not. Life is too short to waste time holding grudges."

"I agree. I'm so sorry I was so disagreeable to you and Jessica. I feel so torn, wanting to help Jessica but wanting to give Gordon my support too. I feel like he really needs it right now." She sighed. "I just hope Gordon and Trace can overcome their differences so we can really be a family."

"They will. Just give them time and keep praying," Kate said, though she wasn't as sure as she sounded. How could the family overcome the cloud of suspicion hanging over Trace unless he cleared his name?

"I've been doing a lot of that lately. Jessica said she's praying too. With all those prayers, something's got to give." She led Kate down the path toward the stables.

"I wish we could stay here this winter, but Gordon insists we have to be on-site while we market the Hawaii property. He seems almost desperate to get that sold. I hope it sells quickly so we can come back here. I want Gordon to stay in one place long enough to relax and recuperate. Every time I mention going in for tests, he says he's fine, but I've noticed things that concern me."

"Like what?"

"Like indigestion and headaches and just general irritability. I wonder if those are signs of an ulcer."

"Maybe. Especially if he's under unusual stress, like worrying about his business. Could he be having problems with a business relationship?" She didn't want to say she'd seen Gordon and Brian arguing, but something was amiss there, and she hoped Monica would provide a clue.

"He and Brian argue sometimes, but that's nothing new. He's had more hassles than usual over our newest endeavor near Bali. This is one of the foreign resorts I told you about that he bought with Brian. It has a wonderful beach, and it was in pretty good condition, but a typhoon caused a lot of damage. It's been closed for over a year. He's made a couple of trips to oversee the repairs, but they have trouble with workers and materials."

"Goodness. I can't even imagine trying to manage something like that long-distance. I suppose there's a language barrier too."

"Yes. And they don't do business the same way we do. They want to haggle over everything. I think Gordon would sell it if they could find a buyer."

They entered the lounge area of the stables. Monica crossed the room and opened the office door. She stopped abruptly and stared.

"What in the world . . ."

Kate nearly ran into her. She looked over Monica's shoulder. Flora and Bertie were standing behind Gordon's desk.

"What are you two doing in here?"

"Why, we're waiting for Mr. Gordon. Why else would we be here?" Flora said, giving Monica an innocent look.

"He's not at home," Monica said, wrinkling her brow. "I'll tell him you're looking for him."

"Please do," Flora said, straightening up. "We'll be on our way then." Flora and Bertie walked to the door, then paused and looked back at Monica before heading off toward the mansion.

"What in the world could they have been doing?" Monica said, looking puzzled. "Flora used to come once in a while to clean the office, but those two looked like I'd caught them doing something wrong, if you ask me."

Monica went to the desk and turned on the computer. Kate stood in the doorway. Glancing at the desk, she noticed one of the file cabinet drawers was open a crack. Had Gordon left it that way? Or had Flora and Bertie left it that way in their hurry to escape?

Chapter Twenty-Four

Kate had just hung up her coat when the phone rang. She went in the kitchen to answer it.

"Hello," she said.

"Kate Hanlon?" a male voice asked. She didn't recognize it.

"Yes."

"This is Art Franklin from Charlottesville, Virginia. I got a message that you wanted to talk to me about Trace Jackson."

"Yes." Kate was so excited, her hands began to shake as she grabbed a pencil and paper. "Thank you for calling. I'm so sorry about your son," she said.

"Oh, thank you. Did you"—he cleared his throat—"did you mention anything to Trace?"

"No. I wanted to speak to you first. I'd better explain why I was trying to find you."

Kate explained about Trace and Jessica and their upcoming wedding, the suspicion about Trace because of the incident at Appomattox Commercial Bank and his recent access into Jessica's bank information, and the strife it was causing with Trace's future family.

Art was silent for several long moments. Finally, with a quiet but steady voice, he spoke. "Trace is innocent of all wrongdoing in that bank mess," Art said. His voice was heavy. "See, he took the heat from the encoding error to protect *me*."

"You?" Kate hadn't expected that revelation.

"Yes." There was a long pause. For a moment Kate thought she'd lost the connection, but then she heard a deep sigh. "I messed up big time. I had a family, and my son had special needs, and I couldn't keep up with the medical bills." There was something almost like fear in his voice. "I set up the encoding error to redirect the money to a nonexistent account, then I sort of borrowed the money to pay the medical bills. I thought . . . I hoped, since it was a relatively small amount of money, it might not be noticed until I could pay it back."

He breathed shakily into the phone. "When the error was discovered, I panicked. I didn't have any money to cover the error. They hadn't found my account—only that the money was missing—but I lost my nerve. I didn't know what to do. Trace is so smart, I confided in him that I'd screwed up, but I didn't tell him where the funds had gone. I told him that I had no idea." There was a pause.

"Trace is a good man. A great man. He took the blame for the error. I didn't want him to do it, but he insisted. He said he was single, so it didn't matter. And I let him. I think we both knew he would get fired, but at the time, it seemed better than losing my job and not being able to take care of Tim . . . of my family. If they'd tracked the money, I'd have confessed, but they didn't." He was silent for a moment. "I never should have let him do it." His voice was full of regret.

Kate couldn't believe what she was hearing. The man

sounded contrite, but how could he have let Trace take the blame for his own crime?

"So what's your situation now?" Kate said, trying to keep her voice calm.

"I work for a different bank. I completed college and got my CPA certification, then I took a job in Charlottesville. I'm the director of risk management. Ironic, isn't it?" The man sighed. "Trace shouldn't have to pay for a stupid and costly decision I made three years ago. I want to help him. What can I do?"

"Clearing Trace will put your job and career in jeopardy, not to mention that you'll likely face criminal charges . . ."

"Yes."

Kate had to admire the man's courage to right his wrong. "Do you have any other children?"

"A little girl. She's seven months old and beautiful. But I need to clear this up, no matter what happens to me. This lie has been eating at me for three years." Art sounded almost determined. "I need to tell Trace about this. And I'd love for him to meet my baby girl, if he'll even talk to me after he finds out. He needs to know about Tim too. They were pals."

"I think he would love that," Kate said quietly. "Art, thank you for being willing to come forward, especially on behalf of Trace. I know that God is eager to forgive if we confess our wrongdoings to him. I think you'll gain as much from your confession as Trace will, even if it means hardship as a result."

"Thank you, Kate. I can't tell you how relieved I feel to get this secret out in the open."

"I can imagine," Kate said. She knew it was easier for people to confess to a perfect stranger, like a pastor or a pastor's wife, especially when he wasn't face-to-face with her, but it was a step in the right direction. "Art, can I have your phone number? I'll leave it up to you to contact Trace"—she gave Trace's phone number to Art—"but I'd like to be able to get in touch with you should something come up."

"Sure thing." He gave her two phone numbers and his new address.

"Thanks for getting in touch, Art. I promise I'll be praying for you and your family. God is faithful." He still had to tell Trace. Would he? Did he have that much courage?

She hung up, relieved that her belief in Trace's innocence proved true, but saddened by Art's dismaying situation. Still, she was hopeful that Art's confession would help Trace's relationship with Gordon.

Yet there was still the matter of Trace's recent attempts at gathering information on Jessica's funds. How could Kate make sense of it all?

She sat at the oak table to think. Trace had never made any encoding error or taken money from the bank. He was wrongly fired. To Kate, that confirmed her theory about the recent inquiry into Jessica's bank records. Trace had the best of motives—Jessica's happiness—at stake.

SUNDAY MORNING, the Mackenzie crew took up two full pews at Faith Briar. Some of Jessica's bridesmaids, including Kristin, and Trace's groomsmen had arrived. Monica and Brian were there too. Only Gordon was missing.

After the service, Trace and Jessica introduced their friends to Paul and Kate. Surrounded by her wedding party and holding hands with her fiancé, Jessica looked happy.

With a busy schedule, a shrunken wedding budget, and nearly half a million dollars yet to be recouped, Jessica still seemed content and excited about her future.

Kate knew that Jessica treasured love and relationships above possessions. Amazing that this girl who'd grown up with limitless wealth and provisions cared so little about material things. She had her priorities right, and Kate felt assured that Jessica and Trace would find happiness whatever their circumstances.

Kate was especially relieved to know that soon enough, the suspicion about Trace as a banking criminal would be lifted.

Kate thought about the upcoming week as she watched the large group exit the church. She knew the time would fly by. The rush of activity would carry them all along to Saturday, with little time to think about trust funds or second thoughts. She said a silent prayer that peace would reign in the midst of all the activity and that somehow Jessica and her father would come together.

Monica hung back until most of the parishioners had left.

"Can you imagine? All of Jessica's friends are staying at the house," Monica said to Kate. "Breakfast was a zoo. It's been too long since I was around so many young women."

"Let wedding week begin!" Kate said with a laugh.

"Exactly . . . It's madness! Trace's family comes in Tuesday. We offered our guesthouse, but they wanted to be near Trace, so they're staying in Pine Ridge."

"They're probably concerned that you have enough extra people staying with you already," Kate said. "I'm sure you and Trace's parents will have plenty of time to get to know each other though."

"I hope so," Monica said. "Getting to know the groom's mother will surely help me understand the groom better."

The pair talked a bit more about wedding plans while Paul greeted the few remaining parishioners. After Monica walked out, Kate turned to Paul. "The wedding is on the fast track now."

"It'll be a busy week for you. Trace asked if we could have another session on Tuesday night. His family arrives that day, and he wanted us to get together with them. Is that all right?"

"That's fine." Kate sighed. "Speaking of . . . I got an interesting call from an old co-worker of Trace's, Art Franklin, the other day." Kate quietly filled Paul in on the details of Art's call.

"Wow," Paul said, looking out as Monica's car pulled out of the parking lot. "I'm glad to hear that we have proof of Trace's innocence, but it's going to be a long road for Art and his family."

"My thoughts exactly," Kate said, nodding. "So how is your sermonette for the ceremony coming along?"

Paul shook his head. "Not well. I've written and deleted several drafts. It still hasn't come together in my mind."

"It will," Kate said. She was hoping a lot more would come together than just Paul's message.

TRACE AND HIS FATHER helped Paul crowd extra chairs into his office Tuesday night. Trace's father and older brother stood well over six feet tall and looked like Norse giants with their thick blond hair, broad shoulders, and large builds. His mother was medium height, a few inches shorter than Trace, but she looked petite next to her husband. Trace's sister and sister-in-law leaned against the wall looking very tired and uncomfortable. They were both in their last trimesters of pregnancy.

Kate wheeled in Millie's chair, which was padded, and brought Paul's padded desk chair around for the pregnant sisters. With Trace's brother-in-law, Jessica, and Paul and Kate, they had a crowd.

After introductions, Jessica and Kate went through the plans for the rehearsal and wedding day and checked to make sure the men had rented their tuxedos. Trace's brother and sister treated the prospective groom to a lot of good-natured teasing, and the meeting became more of a social time than a premarital counseling session. As the guests got tired, the party wound down.

"Four more days, Katie girl. Then it will all be over," Paul said, draping his arm around her shoulder as they walked to the truck.

"I feel nearly as frazzled as if it were Rebecca's wedding," Kate said, speaking of their youngest daughter. Kate thought she would love to orchestrate her wedding someday, but for now, Jessica's wedding would satisfy the wedding bug.

"You weren't frazzled before Melissa's wedding," Paul said.

"Oh yes, I was. You were just too distracted to notice."

Kate was confident that Jessica and Trace's wedding would go smoothly. Every wedding had a glitch or two, but those usually added to the wealth of memories. She regretted that one issue remained unresolved: Jessica's trust fund. If only she could solve that mystery before the wedding, perhaps it would heal the rift between Gordon and Trace and help bring Trace into the family. Kate couldn't think of a more perfect wedding present.

Chapter Twenty-Five

K ate ran errands early Thursday morning. With the wedding and all the preparations, she wouldn't have another
chance until Monday morning. She hadn't even thought about
what she would wear to the ceremony. When she got home
from town, she skimmed through her closet and came up with
a graceful floral georgette skirt and a shell and silk jacket that
had pockets for tissues and incidentals that might be needed.
Dressy but practical, and the outfit was ready to wear.

She checked Paul's side of the closet. Since the groomsmen's tuxedos were charcoal grey, she picked out a black suit
and a gray-, black-, and white-striped tie. She took the suit
out of the plastic cover and hooked the hanger over the door
so the suit would air out.

She sat down with her notebook to make a list of items to
take to the wedding. Needle and spools of white and black
thread, clear tape, safety pins, bandages, Ibuprofen, a glue stick,
rubber bands, extra tissues, a stain-remover stick, hangers.

When the doorbell rang, Kate glanced at her watch. It
was barely noon. Kate looked out through the narrow window

next to the door. A man was standing on the porch. She opened the door.

"Hello?" He was a big man in his midthirties, Kate guessed.

"Are you Kate Hanlon?"

"Yes."

"I'm Art Frank—"

"Oh, Art. Welcome. Please come in. I wasn't expecting you. I'm so glad you came." Kate was rambling. She knew it. She was so flabbergasted, she didn't know what to say. But she was comforted by the look in the man's deep-set eyes—he was there to help Trace.

"My wife and baby are in the car."

Kate looked out past him and waved. "They're welcome to come in. Are you hungry? I can fix y'all some lunch."

His face was flushed. "No, thanks. We had a bite in Pine Ridge. But I'll go get Kim and the baby anyway." He backed up, then turned and went to the car. Kate could see that the baby was asleep. He unhooked her car seat and carried her in.

"Kate, this is my wife, Kim."

"Come in. You must have left Virginia early to get here by noon. Let me get you something to drink. Water? Coffee? Sweet tea?"

"Water would be great." Kim sat on the couch next to the baby carrier. She looked nervous.

"I told Kim everything, and she said we had to come."

Kate handed them glasses of water. "Trace will be so glad to see you. Have you talked to him yet?"

"No, I decided to wait until I could come in person. Did you tell him you talked with me?"

Kate shook her head. "Should I try calling him?" She reached for the cordless phone, resting on the end table.

"Wait. You said Trace's future father-in-law was against the marriage, right?"

"Yes. His name's Gordon."

"Then Gordon's the man I need to speak with. I'll see Trace later. I don't want Trace to argue with me. He already sacrificed so much for me. Even when he hears the truth, he might object to my telling his father-in-law."

"I understand," Kate said. "Gordon and his wife live near here. Would you like to pay them a visit?"

Art looked down at his hands. "That would be good."

"I can take you up there and introduce you. Kim, would you and the baby like to wait here?"

Kim thanked Kate, and Kate went into the kitchen to call Monica. "Is Gordon at home?" she asked.

"We're just having lunch," Monica said, her voice bewildered. "Why?"

"Can I pay you a visit? I have someone here who wants to talk to Gordon. It's very important."

"Sure, Kate. Absolutely. But . . . is everything okay?"

"Yes, everything's as it should be."

Chapter Twenty-Six

Gordon frowned when Kate and Art entered the smaller of the two dining rooms at Gentian Hill Manor, but he quickly hid his consternation and stood to greet them.

"Kate. Nice to see you." He held out his hand to Art. "I'm Gordon Mackenzie."

Kate introduced Art.

Monica raised her eyebrows but smiled and shook his hand. "Please, sit down and join us. Have you had lunch? Can I get you something to drink?"

"No, thanks," Art said.

"Art has come for the wedding," Kate started. "He's an old friend of Trace's." Kate looked at Art, then at Gordon and Monica. "He wants to speak with you. I'll just wait in the other room."

"No, please, stay. Have a seat, both of you," Monica said.

Art and Kate obediently sat down across from Gordon and Monica.

"How nice that you could come," Monica said. She shot Kate a questioning look. No doubt she was mentally scrolling through the guest list and not coming up with Art's name.

"I really made the trip from Virginia to talk to you, Mr. Mackenzie. You see, I used to work with Trace at Appomattox Commercial Bank." Gordon flinched. "We worked in the same department when an encoding error was made that cost the bank a heap of money." Art took a deep breath. Kate could see he was nervous.

Art explained his involvement in the banking fiasco, including the fact that Trace was unaware Art had stolen from the bank, but instead believed that Art had made an honest mistake.

Gordon stared at Art. Monica stared at Art. Finally Gordon found his voice.

"Why in the world would he take the blame for you? He could have ruined his chances of getting another job."

"I had a family. Trace was single. I had a son who had Down syndrome. Trace is a really great guy, Mr. Mackenzie. Your daughter is a very lucky woman to marry him. You're lucky to get him as a son-in-law. He loved my son, and my son loved him. Tim called him Uncle Trace. He coached my son's Special Olympics team." Art paused. "Truth is, I should have come forward with this a long time ago." Art looked at Kate. "Anyway, the Special Olympics is how Kate found me. She searched for the connection and found my son's track team."

Gordon was silent for so long, Kate didn't know what to think. His misconceptions about Trace were going down the drain. She realized that would take some adjustment.

"But that still doesn't explain why Trace was investigating Jessica's bank accounts just last week," Gordon said to Monica. He crossed his arms over his chest. He looked so incredulous, Kate almost felt bad for the guy.

"Actually, I think I can explain that," Kate said. "But please don't tell Jessica. Trace has worked so hard to make it a surprise for her."

Gordon waited for her to go on.

"Trace bought Jessica the house she wanted. Trace must have listed her name on the mortgage papers," Kate said quietly. "The bank would have had to look into her banking history before they would guarantee the loan."

Gordon sat still, clearly dumbfounded.

"But . . ." His voice faltered. "But if Trace loves my daughter so much, why didn't he defend himself? Why didn't he tell me the truth? Wouldn't he put her ahead of any other loyalty? If I'd had my way, I'd have stopped the wedding."

"I'm glad you didn't, sir. My son had serious health problems. Trace knew that. He didn't want to risk my son's future. It was an incredible sacrifice. What Trace doesn't know is that my son passed away nearly six months ago. I'm going to have to tell him about that, and about my guilt for embezzling the bank's money."

Gordon looked shaken by that pronouncement. "I'm sorry. You haven't seen Trace?"

"No sir. I came straight here."

Gordon ran his hand through his hair. "What about you?" He nodded toward Art. "You'll lose your job . . ."

"Yes, and I may even have to serve a prison sentence. Trace had a huge impact on my life with his devotion to Tim. I'd never forgive myself if I came between him and his future family. Either way, I should have spoken up and cleared his reputation a long time ago. But then I found out my wife was pregnant, and . . . well, I'm determined to make it right now, so I plan to tell my boss and my former employer as soon as I return home."

Art stood to go.

"Thank you," Monica said after she stood and shook Art's hand, then hugged Kate. "I don't know what I would have done without you," she whispered in Kate's ear. Kate squeezed the woman tighter in mutual appreciation.

Gordon stood and nodded at Art. He looked worn out.

As Kate and Art walked out to her car, he thanked her. "I'm so glad to tell the truth and clear Trace. I'm almost relieved, actually. Don't get me wrong. I have my family to think of. Kim has forgiven me and promised to stand by me. She says God will get us through this. I don't know how I'll support her and the baby, but I'm ready to confess and do my time." He squared his shoulders. "First, though, I need to get in touch with Trace."

"No problem. We'll give him a call. I'm sure he'll want to see you and your family."

"Thank you. If you hadn't persisted in finding me, I'd still be living under this cloud, and so would Trace."

"I just can't resist a puzzle," she said, smiling. "And the Lord has answered my prayers. I'll pray for you too, Art. Kim is right. Whatever happens, the Lord will walk you through it."

KATE WAS HOME DOING LAUNDRY later that day when the doorbell rang. She barely heard it from the garage. Before she could get to the door, it rang again and again. Someone was desperate.

Kate opened the door. Jessica stood there grinning and bouncing up and down.

"Come in. What's happened?" Kate thought she might have met Art or talked to Monica. "Have you been home?"

Jessica stepped into the house. "No. I came straight here. I'm so excited, I wanted you to be the first to hear. It's the most amazing thing!" she said. "Trace gave me my wedding present early. You'll never guess!" Her hands were balled and pumping up and down like in a victory dance.

Kate knew what was coming, but she didn't want to spoil Jessica's surprise. "Tell me," she said.

"He bought the house! Trace bought me the house. He took me to sign the papers today. I have them in here," she said, patting her large purse. "It's ours! He told me he's been saving for something special for years and years." Tears of excitement were making her blink.

"What a wonderful surprise," Kate said. Obviously Jessica had no concerns about where Trace got his money. She trusted him totally; her father's accusations had not fazed her one bit. Kate knew her trust was warranted, but Jessica didn't know that yet. Her trust in Trace pleased Kate almost as much as her joy over her wedding present.

"Trace took me to see the house again. I can't wait to begin fixing it up."

"If you need help, I can wield a paintbrush, and I bet Monica would like to help too."

"Oh yes! I'll ask her. Maybe she can help me pick out colors, as long as she doesn't get too bright." Jessica laughed. "I'm going home right now to tell her." She threw her arms around Kate for a big hug. "Thank you for everything. I don't know what I'd do without you."

"It's been my pleasure. I have the feeling that the Lord

knew just what he was doing when he brought us together as friends," Kate said with a wink.

Kate watched Jessica bounce down the steps and walk to her car. Trace couldn't have known that Art would come to clear his name with the Mackenzies. And he couldn't have known that Jessica wouldn't learn the truth until she got home. He'd picked the perfect time to reveal his surprise gift, before Jessica had proof of his trustworthiness.

Still, someone around Jessica was not trustworthy. But who?

Who concocted the elaborate network of false organizations to funnel the money, and where did it end up? It had to have gone through banks somewhere.

Kate still had information from Jessica's trustee on the phony investment accounts. On a hunch, Kate got out the papers, then found Art's cell-phone number and called him. As a bank employee, he might be able to help.

Chapter Twenty-Seven

When the phone rang the next day, Kate knew it would be Art returning her call.

"You caught me at just the right time. I looked up the trust-fund information before I told my boss about everything else." He sounded sad but resolved. "Of course, he fired me. But I expected it."

"I'm so sorry, Art."

"It'll be fine. Anyway, about Jessica's trust fund. I looked into the encoding, and it's clear—all the monies from the fund went through the Appomattox Commercial Bank," he said.

Kate was stunned. She hadn't expected that. If Art hadn't already cleared Trace . . . "You're sure?"

"Absolutely. I can't tell you who owns the account, though. That information is well protected. But the addresses on the accounts are definitely bogus. The transaction encoding all leads to the bank."

"I see. Thank you, Art."

"I hope it helps."

"Yes. I hope so too. I'll be praying for you and your family."

After they said their good-byes, Kate's mind swirled with this new information and the possibilities it presented. She sat on her bed, staring across the room. She hadn't seen that coming.

Thank you, Lord, for sending Art. Please have grace and mercy on him and his family. I pray that his repentant spirit will hold sway over the judge and jury, and that his sentence would be minimal.

KATE STOOD in the Gentian Hill Manor mansion, looking out at the beautifully decorated patio. A covered dais with simple columns had been erected at the end of the patio, with the valley and mountains beyond as a spectacular backdrop. Plastic sheeting covered the white-carpeted floor and wide steps in the house to keep them clean until the wedding the following day.

It was the night of the rehearsal, and Kate was standing inside the Mackenzie house with most of the wedding party, trying to make sense of the order of events. Paul and Trace would come out of the formal dining-room doorway at the north end of the house, while the rest of the wedding party would enter the patio from the center doorway.

Gordon and Monica and Trace's parents and grandparents were standing at the back of the room. The groomsmen stood apart from the bridesmaids.

"Okay, girls. Line up in order," Kate said. "Grandparents and parents first, bride and father last. Men, I need three ushers up here."

The four-year-old daughter of one of the bridesmaids was

carrying a basket of dried petals to practice. She was crunching the petals between her fingers, listening to them rustle as they disintegrated.

Kate glanced at Monica and Gordon. Monica's gaze let Kate know they were ready. Gordon looked somber.

The musicians were ready. A baby-grand piano had been wheeled outside next to the dais. Kate called Paul on her cell phone. "We're ready."

"Okay. We're ready here."

Monica gave the pianist a signal. Soft music began. Paul and Trace came out from the side and stood up on the dais.

The procession of bridesmaids and groomsmen began.

Monica watched carefully, giving instructions to slow down and to leave space between them. Next, it was time for the flower girl. The young woman who was helping started out with her, then let her go alone. The child made it to the front, scattering bits of dry petals along the way. Kate looked back at Jessica and Gordon.

Jessica looked excited. Gordon looked sick.

"Relax," she told them. "This is Jessica's big moment, so take it slow. When you get to the front, Paul will ask who gives her away, and then you speak as you hand her over to Trace." She studied Gordon's pallor. "Are you all right?"

"Fine," he answered. "Let's get this over with."

"Okay." She gave the pianist and violinist their signal.

Paul walked through the basics of the ceremony with Trace and Jessica, then it was time for the bride and groom to return down the aisle holding hands. Trace was goofing off, raising their hands in victory and hooting. Jessica was laughing. Then came the bridesmaids and groomsmen and the flower girl. Everyone was laughing and talking, so Kate almost didn't notice when Kristin came up behind her in the hall.

"Kate, I've been thinking about the day you saw me at the pawnshop," she said, keeping her voice low. "I know what you must think. It looks like I've been stealing from Jess, but it's not true. I had to sell some of my things after I got into some credit-card debt, but I love Jess. She's more like a little sister than a cousin to me. I . . . I just wanted to clear that up."

Kristin's eyes looked directly into Kate's, begging Kate to believe her.

"I know that you care deeply for Jessica," Kate said. "She loves you too. And I do believe you. I'm sorry I jumped to a false conclusion at the pawnshop."

"It's okay. I can see why you thought that. Thanks for being such a good friend to Jessica. I'm afraid I haven't been very supportive, but believe it or not, I'm learning from your example."

Kate wasn't sure how to respond, but Kristin quickly gave her a hug, then turned and started up the stairs. Kate watched her go. Out of the corner of her eye, she saw Gordon, looking ashen, go down the side hall toward the den. She followed him. He entered the den, and Kate stepped into the room after him. He went to a desk in the corner and took an envelope out of a drawer, then he put his hand on the desk, leaning down as if in pain.

"Gordon?" she said.

He stiffened. She started to move forward but stopped. He looked over his shoulder at her.

"I'm all right. I'll be out in a minute."

"Do you want me to get Monica?"

"No!"

"Monica is worried about your health."

"There's nothing wrong with my health. She worries too much." He shook his head, beads of sweat on his brow.

"There may not be anything wrong with your health, Gordon, but there's something else weighing you down, isn't there?"

He turned to face her. "You were there with Jessica at Balderson's office." He lowered himself slowly into his desk chair. "I blame myself. I thought Trace was after her money. I was so certain. I was shocked by what that young man said yesterday. And"—he swallowed—"I know I should be relieved that Trace can be trusted."

Kate's eyebrows rose. "But you know Trace isn't the problem."

Gordon sighed. "No, he isn't."

"Why did you take the money, Gordon? Did you need it to cover losses on your horse? Or for the resort near Bali?"

Gordon stood so still, staring at her, Kate wondered if he had turned to stone. She heard a soft noise behind her but didn't look back.

"How did you know about those?"

"It wasn't hard to find out," she said. "And when I learned that all the transfers went through Appomattox Commercial Bank, everything made sense. You knew about Trace's indiscretions with the bank, and you also knew that he would look even guiltier if anyone discovered that the funds had gone through there." Gordon slumped in his chair and put his head in his hands.

"You're going to have to tell Jessica," Kate said. "But she'll forgive you. She loves you."

Gordon shook his head. "Why should she?"

"Because you're her father."

"Some father." He looked up. His gaze went beyond her, and he frowned. "I wanted to protect her. I moved the money to keep it safe."

"But it's not there, is it? That's why you're physically sick over this. You can't return the money."

His features twisted as if in pain. "I'm so sorry," he said.

Kate knew he wasn't talking to her. She heard a movement behind her just before Monica rushed to her husband, who stood and put his arms around her. He collapsed against her.

"It's all right," Monica said. "Gordon, it's all right. We'll get through this."

A deep, agonizing sob broke from Gordon. Kate heard a soft shuffle behind her. She turned. Jessica and Trace stood in the doorway. Jessica's eyes were filled with pain. She started to go to her father, but Trace held her back. She glanced at him, then stopped and leaned against him.

Gordon didn't see her. He was facing Monica. She tried to shush him, but he kept talking, explaining. "I took Jessica's inheritance and blew it. I can't even pay for this wedding."

Monica smoothed her hand over his hair. "It doesn't matter, Gordon. The wedding is taken care of. And we'll sell some of our more expensive valuables. We'll find a way to make this work."

"Don't you understand? I tried to sell one of the resorts to pay for the Bali disaster and pay Jessica back, but the deal fell through. Nothing's moving."

"Daddy?" Jessica stepped out of Trace's embrace and went to her father.

She stood in front of her father, her arms open, beseeching. "Daddy, I love you so much."

"Oh, baby." Gordon moved to his daughter, and he wrapped his arms around her, sobbing. "I'm so sorry. I didn't mean to let you down. Can you ever forgive me?"

"Yes, of course I forgive you." Jessica was crying with her father.

Kate turned away, embarrassed to be witnessing such a private moment.

"I'll never forget how after Mama died, you came to my room every night to read to me until I fell asleep so I wouldn't be scared and lonely." Jessica sniffed and pulled her father closer. "When I went away to school, you called me every week and sent me gifts and flowers and cards so I'd know you loved me. Even after you and Monica got married, you still called me all the time. You spent your life giving me love. That's enough of an inheritance for me. I don't need anything else."

Jessica reached out with one arm and pulled Monica into the embrace. Gordon hugged his two women.

Kate turned to leave. Trace opened the door and stepped out with her.

"Gordon still needs to reconcile with you," Kate said. "Can you ever forgive him?"

Trace didn't even hesitate. "He's Jessica's father. She loves him. Tomorrow, he'll be part of my family. I've already forgiven him."

Their footsteps echoed on the polished marble as Kate

and Trace walked down the hall. "The relationship will come in time. I'm not in a hurry. We'll work it out," Trace said.

"He's fortunate to have you as a son-in-law," Kate said.

Trace waved her comment away. "I'm lucky to have Jessica." He paused. "I didn't get a chance to thank you for contacting Art."

Kate smiled. "It was my pleasure."

"I'm really disappointed in him, but I can see how he rationalized and got into this mess. His willingness to come forward makes it easier for me to forgive him."

Kate was moved by Trace's generosity.

"I didn't know about Tim either," he said. "He was a special kid. He loved everyone, even people who were mean and teased him. I learned a lot from him." Trace's eyes got a far-off look. "Why don't you go ahead to the dinner and tell everyone we'll be there soon," he said at last. "Paul's in the living room waiting for you."

"All right. We'll be praying for you."

"Thanks." Trace surprised Kate with a hug. She hugged him back, then went to find Paul.

Chapter Twenty-Eight

The gold room looked as if a tornado had hit it. Dresses, shoes, makeup bags, curling irons, purses, jeans, shirts, and sweaters were strewn everywhere. The bridesmaids were busy curling each other's hair, repairing nail polish, talking on cell phones, and dancing around to music from a boom box. They had over an hour before the ceremony. Kate left and went downstairs to see how everyone else was doing.

Flora and three ladies were busy in the kitchen, putting the finishing touches on dozens of hors d'oeuvres. The mixture of savory and sweet smells and baking scones made Kate's stomach growl. Flora spotted her and waved her over.

"Here," she said. "This one didn't work. Have a taste."

"It looks perfect to me. The wonderful smells in here are driving me crazy." Kate popped a savory pasty in her mouth. The flaky crust melted on her tongue. "*Mmm*. Good."

Flora beamed. "I offered one to Monica, but she said she's too nervous to eat. Have you seen her? She looks like a queen."

Kate saw the pride in Flora's expression. She was back at the Mackenzie mansion as a member of the clan, and Monica was part of the royalty. Earlier, Kate had helped Bertie and Monica set out dozens of roses in full bloom around the patio.

So far, everything was on schedule with no major glitches.

Jessica and Trace had shown up a little late for the rehearsal dinner, but no one seemed to notice. Monica and Gordon came late and only stayed a short time. Brian and several business associates attended, and they hit it off with Trace's father and brother.

Kate had made a point to approach Brian about the resorts and ask how he was handling the stress. Brian confided that he had tried refinancing his ranch for capital to rebuild the Bali resort, but his liability as a partner had nixed that deal. The argument Kate had witnessed before really had been tension between Brian and Gordon as they'd tried to work through their financial problems.

Kate had also noticed during her conversation with Brian that Kristin kept glancing his way from across the room. Eventually the young woman walked over to them. Brian excused himself from conversation with Kate and gave Kristin his attention. The party was a smashing success.

As Kate looked around the Mackenzie home on the wedding day, things seemed to be running smoothly and on schedule. Kate took a moment to call Paul, who was still at home.

"Are you ready?" she asked him.

"Just put the last touches on my message. I'm dressed and ready to leave."

"I'm so glad you were finally able to move beyond your sermon-writer's block," Kate said.

"Ugh. Me too. I sure had my share of worries over it, didn't I?"

"You did, but not I," Kate said. "I had no doubt you'd pull through." She laughed. "See you in a few minutes."

GUESTS WERE STEADILY TRICKLING IN. Monica had hired parking attendants and had turned the pasture into a lot. Bertie was helping Flora and the ladies in the kitchen.

As Kate watched from inside the mansion, Renee fluttered in with Kisses tucked under her arm.

"Oh, look at how lovely it all is," she said. She wasn't sure if Renee was addressing her or the world at large. "Monica was wise to take so much of my advice—I do have exquisite taste. Of course, Monica's sense of style is almost as good as mine."

Kate gave Renee a warm smile, and the older woman continued through the house, off to observe her masterwork, Kate assumed.

As Kate made her way up the stairs to check on the bridesmaids, Monica came down.

"You look beautiful," Kate said.

Monica was wearing the silver dress she'd bought from the New York designer. Her hair was swept up on one side, held in back with a jeweled clip and curling over her other shoulder.

"Thank you." She took a deep breath. "I feel like a wreck."

"Nervous?"

Monica held out her hand. It was shaking a little.

Kate took her hand and held it still. "Everything is right on schedule. In two hours, it'll be over, and you'll be enjoying your guests."

Monica smiled. "I'll keep reminding myself of that."

"Good. How's Gordon?"

"Oh, not good. You'd think he'd be relieved, but he feels so bad, he doesn't want to face anyone. I barely got him to the rehearsal dinner. Did you know why he went to the den last night? He went to get a letter for Jessica that her mother had left for her wedding day."

"Oh wow. I saw him take an envelope out of the desk. How special."

"He was sick over giving it to her when he'd failed her so badly. That's why Flora and Bertie were in his office. He'd had them looking for it since he knew how much they loved Amelia and would want to be a part of sharing the letter. I guess they weren't sure whether they should tell us about it when we found them in Gordon's office."

"Ah, that makes sense." Kate paused a moment. "Might it help Gordon feel better if I send Paul to talk to him?"

"It might. He's down at his office by the stables."

"All right. Paul will be here soon."

Monica went on downstairs. Kate went up to the gold room to check on the bridesmaids.

PAUL KNOCKED on the office door at the stables.

"Yes. Come in."

"Gordon, I wanted to see how you're doing." Paul stepped into the office. "Giving your daughter away is a big deal. I remember. I was a basket case the day our oldest daughter got married."

"I bet you didn't mess up her life first," Gordon said.

"Is that what you think?" Paul sat down on a chair across from Gordon. "You know, I've been meeting with your daughter and Trace for the past two months, and I'd say your daughter is a very well-adjusted, happy, generous woman." Paul thought for a moment, then shook his head. "Nope. I can't see anything messed up about her life."

Gordon shifted in his chair. "That's more thanks to her mother's influence than mine, I'm afraid."

"Gordon, I know it's hard to remember this in the thick of a struggle, but fortunes—and sometimes people—come and go. Like Jessica's mother. For some reason, the Lord called her home. Yet through that, Jessica learned to put her trust in the Lord, and he's carried her burdens through everything else along the way, including financial trouble."

There was a tap on the door, and Trace poked his head in. "Can I come in?" He didn't wait for an invitation.

Paul started to leave.

"Wait, Pastor. I need you here," Trace said. He turned to Gordon.

"Sir, a while back I asked for your blessing to marry your daughter. I understand why you denied me. But it'd mean the world to me and Jessica if you'd reconsider."

Gordon looked stunned. "After what I've done, you want my blessing?"

"Yes sir. I'd be honored if you'd consent to having me as a son-in-law, and maybe Pastor Paul would pray for us."

Gordon pushed slowly to his feet. He offered his hand to Trace. "Son, after what I've put you through, if you'd give me your blessing to be your father-in-law, I'd be forever grateful."

Trace ignored Gordon's hand, went around the desk, and embraced Jessica's father. Then he turned to Paul.

"Pastor, would you do us the honor?"

"I'd be happy to."

KATE WATCHED as the maid of honor and the best man walked slowly down the aisle. The flower girl was hopping up and down, waiting for her turn. Fragrant rose petals, fresh from Bertie's collection, spilled out of the basket she held as she bounced around.

Jessica giggled as she watched the flower girl take tiny steps down the aisle, tossing petals into the air. It was a good thing the basket was full.

Kate looked back at Jessica and Gordon. Jessica was radiant in her mother's wedding dress. Her father looked shell-shocked. She snuggled close to his side, and he planted a kiss on her cheek.

"Ready?" Kate asked.

Jessica nodded. Gordon took a deep breath.

"Ready," he said.

Kate raised her hand. The wedding march began. Monica stood from the front row and faced them. Then Trace's family stood, and all the guests rose to their feet, watching for a glimpse of the bride. Paul stood up on the dais, tall and handsome in his suit. Beside him, Trace watched for his bride.

Jessica held her father's arm and slowly swept her way down the aisle. Kate wished she could see her face, but she knew Jessica was beaming. When they got to the end of the aisle next to Monica, Trace stepped down toward them.

"Who gives this woman in holy matrimony?" Paul asked.

"Her mother and I," Gordon said loud and clear.

Monica's hand went to her mouth. Gordon relinquished Jessica to Trace and went to stand beside Monica. Trace took Jessica's hand and led her up the steps to Paul.

The late-afternoon sun shined against the tulle drapes and brilliant roses around the platform and columns, making the display shimmer like a heavenly benediction on the bridal party.

Paul's voice sounded rich, deep as he blessed the couple and all their family and friends. The ceremony was beautiful. Just perfect. Kate remembered their own wedding, how deeply she'd loved the man who had stood beside her that day . . . how much she loved him still.

Jessica recited her vows, then Trace's voice, strong and sure, rang out.

"I, Trace, take you, Jessica, to be my wife, my love, my best friend, to have and to hold from this day forward. I vow to stand beside you and support you in good times and in hard times, to comfort you in sorrow and rejoice with you in joy; for richer, for poorer, in sickness and in health, to love and to cherish; until death do us part."

Kate took a tissue out of her pocket and wiped a tear from her eyes. She wasn't always so emotional, but this wedding held a very special place in her heart. After all they'd been through together, Jessica and Trace were going to be just fine.

About the Author

SUNNI JEFFERS calls a small farm set in remote northeast Washington State home. She loves spending time with her granddaughters and watching out her office window as hawks and eagles soar, and elk, deer, bear, moose and the occasional buffalo stop by the hay fields and forest for a munch. Sunni writes full-time and has won the Romance Writers of America Golden Heart, American Christian Fiction Writers Book of the Year and the Colorado Romance Writer's Award of Excellence.

A Note from the Editors

THIS ORIGINAL BOOK was created by the Books and Inspirational Media Division of Guideposts, the world's leading inspirational publisher. Founded in 1945 by Dr. Norman Vincent Peale and Ruth Stafford Peale, Guideposts helps people from all walks of life achieve their maximum personal and spiritual potential. Guideposts is committed to communicating positive, faith-filled principles for people everywhere to use in successful daily living.

Our publications include award-winning magazines such as *Guideposts* and *Angels on Earth*, best-selling books, and outreach services that demonstrate what can happen when faith and positive thinking are applied in day-to-day life.

For more information, visit us at www.guideposts.com, call (800) 431-2344 or write Guideposts, PO Box 5815, Harlan, Iowa 51593.